Lucky Bet

By

Trish Collins

Books by
Trish Collins
~ ~ ~ ~ ~

Lucky Series

Lucky Day

Lucky Charm

Lucky Break

Lucky Rescue

Lucky Shot

Lucky Honeymoon

Lucky Me

Lucky Number

Lucky Guy

Lucky Couple

Lucky Bet

Lucky O'Shea's - TBA

Jacobs Series

Riptides of Love

Book 1 – Parts 1 & 2

Love's Dangerous
Undercurrents

Book 2 – Parts 1 & 2

Breaking Waves of Love

Book 3 – Parts 1 & 2

Love's Storm Surge

Book 4 – Parts 1 & 2

Impact Zone of Love

Book 5- Parts 1 & 2

Love's Sunset-TBA

{1}

The O'Shea household finally settled down after all the commotion after Tane's dad suffered a heart attack. Tane watched as his father and brothers tore out the wall in the dining room to make the room bigger. There didn't seem to be anything wrong with his father. He looked just as strong and healthy as he always did.

His parents were about to go on their first vacation alone. He would have the entire house to himself for ten full days. Tane didn't think life could get any better. Oh, his mother fussed about him being able to feed himself leading up to them leaving, and he pointed out that he would be off at college in a few short weeks. He would be in big trouble if he couldn't make himself something to eat. Besides, Tane pointed out he could always go to the pub if he got hungry for a real meal.

Arlene yelled up the stairs, "Tane, we're leaving. Please come and say goodbye."

Tane went downstairs to see his brother Mack and his wife Julia standing by the front door. They were waiting to take his parents to the port to get on their cruise ship. Tane hugged his mother.

Arlene pulled back and said, "Are you sure you'll be alright? You know you could stay with Raylan. The keys to my car are on the hook by the door. I feel like I'm forgetting something. I have meals in the freezer."

"Arlene, leave the boy alone. He'll be fine. He is an adult. You were married at his age." Cadman gave Tane a sideways hug. "Don't get into any trouble." His father laughed because out of all the O'Shea clan, Tane was the least trouble.

"Have fun," Tane watched as his parents walked out the door.

Once the door shut and his parents were gone, the house was just how he liked it. Quiet. Tane went up to his room and, instead of listening to his music through his headphones as he always did. He blasted it. "Oh, yeah." Next, he slipped off his pants and threw on an old t-shirt. Tane went back downstairs in his boxers. That was something that he could never do before.

Tane went to the freezer and got the ice cream. He scooped a heaping spoonful into a bowl and moved into the living room, sitting on the couch, listening to his music as he ate. With no one home, Tane put his bare feet on the coffee table, something he wouldn't get caught dead doing if his mother was around. "This is the best vacation ever. My parents can stay on some fancy ship while I get to do what I want." It didn't escape Tane that he'd have to replace the ice cream before his mother got home. He switched on the TV. *Yep, this is great. I might go and turn on every light in the house.* Tane laughed at the thought.

Now, he knew his family members would stop by. Most likely unannounced. He didn't expect to see Mack, Bryant, Paul, or Grace. Ray would come by to check on him, and the twins, Patrick, and Gabe, would come to do their laundry. Now that they had graduated, they were living with their girlfriends. Plus, it would be a great opportunity to push him around. Well, Gabe would be the one to give him a hard time. He was a jerk to everyone except for Faith. Ava could stop by too, most likely to get more of her stuff. She moved into her dorm room early because she decided to take a few courses over the summer.

Tane still had to work at the pub. He finally moved up from dishwasher to server. He thought Mack would never let him turn in his rubber gloves and boots. "I don't miss that job. Too bad I'm heading off to college. Most likely, that's why Mack hired someone else to wash the dishes." Tane shook his head and took his empty bowl into the kitchen. "I'm going to miss having cash in my pocket." Just as he was about to put the bowl in the clean sink. Tane knew it wouldn't take long for the sink to get full, so he rinsed the bowl, putting it in the dishwasher. He wasn't a complete slob.

Tane went upstairs, leaving the TV on. He had to shower before heading to the pub for his shift. Tane went into his room to get his clothes and remembered he didn't need to bring his stuff into the bathroom. Tane smiled, "Being home alone is going to be great." A thought crossed his mind as he walked down the hall. *I could use Mom and Dad's shower. No one would know.* Tane thought better of it and went into the main bathroom. *Besides, all my stuff is in here.* Tane stripped and turned on the water. After he went through the motions, he quickly dried off, leaving his clothes on the floor. He went to his room. It felt so free to be completely naked without a care in the world.

Tane hopped on his bed, laid out, and let the overhead fan dry him the rest of the way. He closed his eyes with his hands behind his head. "I could get used to this." As he relaxed, her image came to him. The scene where he kissed Bailey played in his head. It was as if he could feel her body pressed against his. He tasted her as their tongues tangled with each other. Tane's eyes popped open, "I was dreaming. I did not kiss her. So how could I taste her, or anything else for that matter? I have to stop thinking about her."

Tane got off his bed and pulled an O'Shea's Irish Pub and Grill t-shirt from his drawer, pulling it over his head. "Why am I thinking of her all the time." He slipped into a pair of boxers and jeans. "I know she likes me, but I need to tell her my future plans. That should set the record straight. Then she'll know, and I can get her out of my head." *I hope that works. It didn't seem to deter Bailey in my dream when I told her I was becoming a priest.* "It has to work. I might need to talk to Uncle Joe to see if he could help me."

He turned off his music, went downstairs, and did the same to the TV. The house was quiet again. Tane grabbed his mother's keys off the hook by the back door. "No taking the bus for me. I get to drive to work. This vacation just keeps getting better and better." Tane threw the keys in the air and caught them. "Yes, it is." He jerked his head to the side to get his hair out of his eyes. "I need a haircut." Tane was the only one in the O'Shea clan to have blonde hair. Well, his dad once had a blondish color, but it had turned mostly gray, and his brother Mack had lighter-colored hair.

Tane parked his mother's car next to his sister Ray's in the alleyway behind the pub. He arrived a little early to get something to eat before his shift. Tane was surprised to see Herb working the grill when he walked in the back door. "Hey, Herb. Where's my sister?"

The older man who helped his sister in the kitchen turned, "Oh, she's out there with the girls planning Julia's baby shower."

"Okay, can I get an Everything Burger and fries? How's the new guy working out?"

Herb knew Tane was talking about the new dishwasher. "He's a little slow, but I think he's catching on."

Tane laughed, "Yeah, you get pretty fast when you have three years of experience. It's not a hard job."

"It sure does get hectic when we get busy."

"He'll catch on. Who's working with me tonight?"

"Gabe is behind the bar, and Faith is working the floor."

"So, it's just me and Faith?"

"I'm not sure if anyone else is coming in."

"Thanks," Tane went through the double swing doors to sit at the bar. He said to his brother, "Can I get a soda?"

"That will be two fifty." Gabe got the drink and put it in front of Tane.

"I'm not paying for the drink."

"That's my tip," Gabe said.

"I'm not tipping you either." Tane turned to look around, "Not too busy tonight."

"We don't say that out here because you'll jinx us." Gabe leaned on the bar when Faith walked up to join them. "Do the girls need more drinks?"

Faith smiled, "Yes, everyone needs refills. I hate that I can't be part of the planning party."

Tane said, "After I eat my burger, I'll take over so you can hang with the girls."

"Thanks, Tane." Faith leaned in and kissed him on the cheek. His face turned red. "Are you blushing?"

"No!" Tane jumped off his stool and went into the kitchen.

Faith smiled, "I think that is the most your brother has ever said to me."

"And probably his first kiss, too," Gabe laughed.

"You're kidding, right?" When Faith saw Gabe wasn't joking, she said, "OMG, I didn't even think. I know you all bust his chops about becoming a priest, but."

5

"He is going to be a priest. We weren't kidding about that. Tane hasn't had so much of a girlfriend, much less a kiss."

"Wow, what a waste."

Gabe looked confused, "What do you mean, a waste?"

"He's so cute. I bet all the girls go nuts over him."

Gabe shook his head, "I doubt he'd even notice. Tane keeps to himself. If a girl came up to talk to him, I could see him just standing there and not saying a word."

"I think Bailey has a crush on him."

"Really? Maybe we could have some fun with Tane."

"Gabe, leave it alone. Don't be a jerk."

"That's what I do best."

Faith's brow raised, "Is that what you think you're best at?" Gabe grinned, and Faith walked away to take care of her customers.

Tane grabbed his burger, looking out into the bar to see if Faith was still talking to his brother. She was across the room, so Tane retook his barstool. Gabe was busy at the other end of the bar, and Tane was glad he didn't have to deal with his brother. After finishing his dinner, Tane punched in and got his apron. He waved to Faith to let her know she could go into the back room.

Tane went to his first table, "Hi, I'm Tane. I'll be taking your order. What can I get you to drink?" He didn't bother to write it down because he could remember it. "I'll be back with your drinks." Tane worked the bar area, clearing Faith's tables, and stuffed her tips into his back pocket to keep them separate from his. He looked around, and his tables were all good, so he went to the back room and stopped short when he saw Bailey sitting at the table. Tane quickly recovered and tried to act normal. It made sense that Bailey would be helping with her aunt's baby shower.

"Do you girls need anything?" Tane began picking up empty drink glasses and plates. As he moved around the table, he was extra careful not to touch Bailey as he took her glass. She looked up at him and asked if she could get another soda. "Sure thing. Anyone else?" Tane quickly moved away from her. No one else spoke up, so he carried the dirty dishes into the kitchen. It was nice to just leave them outside the dishwashing room. He went to fill Bailey's drink.

Tane took a deep breath as he returned to the back room. The girls were all talking. He slipped Bailey's drink onto the table and moved out of the room. Tane could have sworn he felt her eyes on him as he left the room or was that wishful thinking. He stopped walking when he realized that he wanted Bailey's attention. This was wrong on so many levels.

When Tane returned to the bar, his brother Mack and his wife, Julia, came from the kitchen. Tane made a U-turn and went to tell his sister that Julia was there. He moved through the opening and said, "Ray, Julia just walked in."

"Oh, crap," Ray started picking everything up off the table. Faith left the room, leaving everyone else to clean up. Grace, Ava, and Bailey quickly moved to put the stuff in Macy's diaper bag. Macy went out by the bar to talk to Julia and distract her. They didn't want Julia to notice everyone coming from the back room at the same time, so Ray went first. She acted as if she had come from the restroom. Raylan said hello and went back into the kitchen. Next, Grace moved out and acted as if she was working. That left Ava and Bailey still in the back room. They stood there trying to think of a way to leave without raising suspicion.

Bailey said, "I can't leave without my aunt knowing something's up, but you work here. I'll wait here until she leaves."

Ava glanced out the door, "Maybe we can get Julia in the kitchen, and you can sneak out."

7

"Okay, that just might work." Bailey watched as Ava left the room. She walked up to her brother Mack and whispered something into his ear. Mack glanced toward the back room and then spoke to his wife. Once Mack got her aunt out of the bar area, Bailey made her move. She rushed by Tane and out the front door.

Tane watched as Bailey bolted by him without even a word. He knew what was happening, yet somehow, he was disappointed. Tane shook off the feeling and went back to work. The rest of his shift was uneventful. Tane punched out and went home to the empty house. He headed upstairs for another shower.

When Tane climbed into his bed, his thoughts went to her. It was times like this when he couldn't stop his mind from going places it shouldn't. The fact that Bailey didn't seem the least bit interested in him bothered him. He didn't catch her watching him. When she asked for her drink refill, Bailey just glanced up at him. No matter how many times he told himself that was a good thing, it didn't feel like it.

Tane closed his eyes, "I just need some sleep, and hopefully, I won't dream about her." That's when his subconscious would take over, and he couldn't control it. The dreams of kissing her lips and having her body up against his made him feel guilty and excited. Tane's last thought was how he needed to speak with his uncle Joe.

Tane didn't know where he was, but she was there, wearing a skimpy top and shorts. Tane wasn't sure if she was wearing a bra because he could see her nipples. His eyes zeroed in on her chest as he watched her. Tane felt his body react. He didn't know if she knew he was there. She certainly didn't act as if she saw him. This gave him time to let his eyes take her all in from top to bottom without her knowing it.

Bailey's hair was in two little braids that gave him a clear view of her neck. The one he wanted to be kissing on his way down her body. She danced around, shaking her cute little ass. Tane wanted to get his hands on her round cheeks so he could pull her into his body. Oh, yeah, rub his cock on her…

Bailey turned as if he had spoken aloud, and her eyes raked over his body. The sensation of her sensual stare washed over his skin. Bailey raised her hand, so her finger touched her lips. She slowly glided it along her bottom lip as if she were thinking about what she was going to do. Bailey walked toward him and reached up to put her arms around his neck.

Tane pushed Bailey against the brick wall in the alleyway. He didn't know how they got there and didn't care. His hands were around her tiny waist as his mouth smashed onto her lips. As their tongues tangled, Tane's fingers itched to touch more of her body. His hands moved up over her ribcage. Tane's thumbs brushed over her hard nipples. He was harder than he'd ever been and wanted to sink his cock deep inside her body. Bailey tried to press her lower body against him, but she was too short. Tane reached down to grab hold of her ass, lifting her so their bodies aligned. He shamelessly rubbed his dick on her pussy. Tane was so close to heaven. It was when his body let loose that Tane woke up to a handful of slime. "Hell," he withdrew his hand from his boxers. Tane got out of bed, trying not to make a bigger mess. "What the hell is the matter with me?" He went to the bathroom and turned on the shower, kicking off his boxers into the pile of clothes he had left on the floor earlier.

Tane let the hot water run over his body. He leaned his hand on the wall with his eyes closed. "I have to stop this. God, if you are testing me. I swear." The dream felt so real, and it left him wanting more. But he knew it was wrong.

After he washed up, Tane didn't want to fall back to sleep for fear he would dream of her. He went downstairs and got himself a bowl of cereal. Tane plopped down on the couch and turned on the TV. As he flipped through the channels, his mind went back to his dream. "No, don't go there. There has to be something on this TV to take my mind off her." He put on a true crime show. Tane figured a "who done it" program would hold his attention.

Once Tane finished his cereal and spread out on the couch. With his arms folded over his chest, he watched the show. It wasn't long before his eyes became heavy. Morning came, and Tane woke to the sound of the phone. He rushed into the kitchen to answer it, "Hello."

"How's single life treating you?" Tane was surprised to hear his uncle's voice on the other end of the line.

"So far, it's good."

"That didn't sound very convincing."

"I didn't sleep well, that's all. Uncle Joe, do you have some time to see me today?"

"I'm sure that can be arranged. Let me look at my schedule. Is lunchtime good for you?"

"That'll work."

"So, what's on your mind?"

"I'd rather speak to you in person."

"Sounds serious. Is everything alright?"

"If you mean, am I in any trouble? No. Well, not the way you might think."

"Okay, then I will see you at noon."

"Thanks, Uncle Joe."

"My pleasure," the line went dead.

Tane took a deep breath because he was about to confess his dreams of Bailey to his uncle. He wasn't proud of it because he thought he should have better control over his thoughts, even though he was sleeping. No matter how much Tane wanted to suppress thoughts of Bailey, he knew something drew him to her. *Was it because she was the first girl, he ever noticed watching him? Or could it be that Bailey was cute as hell? Was it the way she carried herself? She was confident enough to dance at his brother's wedding when no one else was. Yeah, and you were right there watching her.* Tane shook off those thoughts. He'd speak to his uncle. *Hopefully, Uncle Joe will know how to fix this.* Tane got dressed and cleaned his mess from the night before, taking his sheets off his bed. He threw them into the washing machine.

Tane drove to the church and sat in his mother's car for as long as he could. He walked into the church office. All the ladies that worked there knew him.

{2}

Margie was sitting at the front desk today. Tane gave her a little wave as she stood to open the sliding window.

"Well, well, look who we have here, the youngest O'Shea boy. I think you get more handsome every time you come in here."

"I think you may need to see your Optometrist." Margie waved her hand at Tane.

"Smart too. You O'Shea's have good genes."

"Is my uncle in?"

"Oh, yes. Come on in." Margie pushed the button to unlock the door. Tane walked by all the other ladies who worked in the office. He tried not to make eye contact and made a B-line to his uncle's office. He stood outside the door for a few seconds to gather his nerve. After taking a cleansing breath, Tane knocked.

"Come in."

"Hey, Uncle Joe." Tane took the seat on the other side of his uncle's desk.

"What's on your mind, Tane?"

"I need your help."

"What can I do for you?"

"What I'm about to tell you goes no further than this room, right?"

"You know how this works. If this is a confession? Then yes, it stays right here, but if it's not a confession, and I think someone should know, then there are no guarantees."

"Fine, then it's a confession." Tane thought that might be the better way to go. "In the name of the Father, Son, and Holy Spirit, Amen." Tane made the sign of the cross, "Bless me, Father, for I have sinned. It has been one week since my last confession." Tane looked down at his hands folded in his lap. "I've had impure thoughts about a girl. I've tried to control them, but I've been dreaming about her. I have not acted on these thoughts. But it's getting harder and harder to stop them. You know I have committed myself to the Lord. I want my body and soul to be pure, but I fear I'm faltering."

"You know, Tane, there are many priests that have had normal lives before becoming a priest. It is not required to be pure, as you say, just free from sin."

"Uncle Joe, I'm having sexual dreams about her. I don't want to fall asleep. You managed to make it without kissing a girl. Why can't I?"

Joe smiled, "Let me tell you a story. In my senior year of high school, there was this new girl. She was very pretty to look at, but someone very close to me saw her first. As much as I would have liked to ask her out, I kept my feelings to myself. She was unsure how she felt about the other boy because she had never had a boyfriend. This girl asked me to kiss her so she could tell if her feelings toward the other boy were true. Tane, I wanted to kiss her. I thought about it a lot. In the end, she realized that by kissing me would destroy what she and the other boy had. I went off to college, and they got married."

"Do you ever see them?"

"I see them all the time. The girl and I are very good friends. Some things are meant to be, and others are not."

"So, what do I do? How do I get this girl out of my head? I've never even thought about someone like this before."

"Tane, you know what we want and what God has planned for us might be very different. These dreams could be God's way of saying he wants you to go another way."

Tane's eyes got big, "I don't think God would ever condone these types of dreams. They are very sexual in nature. I just want to go off to college like you and forget about her."

"That's not so easily done. You do know there are many other roles you can fulfill in the church and still have a wife and children."

"I think God is testing me with temptation. I have to figure out a way to move past her and get back on track."

"I'm afraid you have a hard road ahead of you."

"I might as well start right now. Give me my penance. I need to pray over this." Tane then said the Act of Contrition, and Father Joe gave Tane his list of prayers and how many times he had to say each one. Joe said the prayer of absolution, taking away his sins. Tane left his uncle's office and went to the church. He sure as hell hoped this worked to free him of the dreams he was having.

Tane walked to the front of the church, sitting in the pew his family sat every Sunday for Mass. He pulled down the kneeling bench and went to his knees. As Tane tried to stay focused on the prayers, in the back of his mind, he wondered if this would work. It had to. He decided every time thoughts of Bailey came into his mind. He'd repeat the penance.

14

Once Tane thought he had a handle on things, he drove home. Sitting around the house wouldn't help his case, so Tane went to his room and got his earbuds. He planned to do some yard work to keep his mind occupied. Tane went outside and pulled the lawnmower out of the garage. It was a hot day, but he figured it would be a good workout. Living in the outer boroughs, his parent's house had property. It was great to have a party, like when they had Raylan and Jon's baby reveal, Mack and Julia's wedding reception, and snowball fights. But pushing a lawnmower over the yard wasn't fun. He figured the hard work would be part of his punishment.

Tane worked the mower over the grass and listened to the music playing in his ears. When he began to sweat, he pulled his shirt off and wiped his face and neck. Throwing it over his shoulder, he kept moving. As Tane's hair got wet from sweat, it made keeping it out of his eyes harder. He shifted his head to the side to move the blonde strands.

When Tane managed to get the backyard cut, he thought the front would have to wait for another day. After putting away the lawnmower, Tane went inside for something to drink. He kicked off his dirty sneakers just as he realized those were his new shoes. "Crap, I should have changed into my old sneakers." He picked them up and threw them into the washer along with his shirt. "I'll wash them after I take a shower."

Tane went to the fridge to get something to drink. He poured himself some iced tea. After taking a few big gulps, he held the glass to his forehead. "Ahhh, it is hot out there." Just then, the doorbell rang. "Who the heck is that?" Tane knew it wasn't anyone who normally came to the house because no one used the front door or rang the bell. "It must be someone trying to sell something." When Tane opened the door, he was shocked to see Bailey standing there. "What are YOU doing here?" His tone wasn't friendly.

Bailey didn't expect to see Tane, much less shirtless. Once she recovered, she raised her chin and said, "Well, hello to you too. I'm here to drop off decorations for my aunt's baby shower," she held up the bags in her hands, "Raylan told me to put them in your mother's sewing room." Bailey sidestepped Tane and started up the stairs.

"Wait, you can't go up there. I'll take them." He followed her as Bailey paid him no mind, and that's when he noticed the short skirt she was wearing. Her butt was just the right height to catch his eye. "You aren't allowed upstairs."

"Don't be silly. I've been up here many times." Bailey walked down the hall."

Tane glanced into the bathroom, quickly closing the door so Bailey didn't see his clothes on the floor. "Yes, that was when there was someone home." Tane put his hands up on the door jamb of his mother's sewing room.

Bailey laughed as she turned to face Tane. "It's not like anything is going to happen. You don't even like me. Anyway, it's fine because I'm over you. You'll only have to deal with me at weddings where we have that one dance together. I might even bring a date to the next one."

"So, you're over me?" Tane sounded as if he didn't believe her.

"Yes, you are far too unsociable for me. I looked at your social media page, and you have like two friends."

"I don't even go on there anymore, and why were you checking me out if you're over me?"

Bailey noticed that Tane was blocking her way. "That was a long time ago. Besides, I only need someone telling me to get out once."

"I didn't know you were there. If you wanted to talk to me, you should have knocked instead of spying on me. It's creepy."

"Well, you don't need to worry. I won't bother to say a word to you." She started for the door, but Tane didn't move. Bailey stepped right up to him. "I think you're in my way."

"So, it seems. What do you say we try to be friends? I don't know much about you, and you don't know me. Our families are forever tied together, and we will see each other a lot. I'd rather be friendly than avoid one another."

"Okay, what do you propose we do to get to know one another?"

"I'm about to order a pizza and watch a movie. Would you like to join me?"

"Stay, now? With no one home?"

"As you said before, nothing's going to happen. What do you say?"

"Where is everyone anyway?"

Tane put his arms down, turning to go back downstairs, "My parents are on a cruise. Ava is living on campus. So, I'm home all alone for nine more glorious days. I never get the house to myself."

"My parents work all the time, so I'm always alone."

"See, we're learning about each other. You're an only child, while I have a bunch of siblings."

"I think this is the most I've ever heard you speak."

Tane smiled, "Once again, when you come from a family like mine, you can't get a word in edgewise." Tane turned to face Bailey, "I don't feel the need to fill the air with meaningless words."

"Now, I'm just the opposite. You like to talk to people when you're alone as much as I am."

"I have to shower. I just got done cutting the lawn. Why don't you order the pizza, and have it delivered? I'll pay for it when it comes."

Bailey yelled after Tane, "What's your address? And what do you want on your pizza?"

Tane yelled down his address and told her he'd eat whatever she ordered. Then said, "Make it an extra-large." Tane waited until he stepped into the shower to ask himself what the hell he was doing. *You're supposed to be not thinking about her, not inviting her to hang out. And most definitely, you should not be noticing her cute ass swaying in that short skirt.* "Ah, hell. I'm in trouble."

Bailey did a happy dance around the room. Not only was Tane talking to her, but he invited her to stay. *Now, play it cool just like you did upstairs. I can't let him know I was bluffing about bringing a date to the next O'Shea wedding.* There were lots of guys that would go with her. But Tane was the one she liked. *You better order the pizza before he comes down."* Bailey quickly pulled out her phone and Googled the nearest pizza place. Once she had placed the order, she sat on the couch to wait for Tane. She closed her eyes and rested her head on the back of the couch. The image of Tane opening the door played in her mind. Now she knew he had a patch of chest hair and just how skinny he was.

Bailey knew Tane was tall and lanky, *but oh, his pants hung so low on his hips. I wonder what it would be like to run my fingers through his chest hair, then work my way down...*

"You didn't fall asleep on me now, did you?" The sound of Tane's voice pulled her from her daydream.

"Nope, just waiting on you." When Bailey opened her eyes, Tane was fully dressed. It was such a shame because he was so yummy before.

"Did you pick a movie? I have every streaming channel there is."

"I didn't even look."

Tane made sure to sit at the other end of the sofa as he turned on the TV. "What kind of movies do you like?" He told himself he'd be

18

okay if he didn't touch Bailey. "Tell me when you see something you want to watch."

"I guess anything you want to watch is fine."

Tane picked a movie and sat back. After fifteen minutes, he glanced Bailey's way, and she looked bored. For the first time in his life, the silence bothered him. Normally, he felt at peace with the calm. But now, he sensed the need to say something, anything.

Bailey stood and said, "Tane."

The doorbell rang and saved him from hearing what she had to say. "That's the pizza." Tane went to the door and paid the delivery driver. "What do you want to drink? I'm sorry, I don't have much to offer you." Tane put the box on the stove. His iced tea sat on the counter from earlier. He opened the fridge as if he didn't know what they had. "I have iced tea, water, or beer."

"Can we split a beer?"

Tane glanced her way over the refrigerator door. "Are you serious? We're both underage. And you're driving."

"I don't think half a beer will affect me. Besides, if I stay for a little while, the alcohol will be out of my system. It's not my first drink."

"Really," Tane took one of the bottles out and twisted off the top. He flipped his hair out of his face. "Do you want a glass?"

"We could share it. No sense in dirtying dishes, right?" Bailey took the bottle from his hand.

Tane opened the pizza box and was surprised to see that Bailey ordered everything on the pie. "So, no plates?"

She moved up to his side and reached around him to get herself a slice. "I think we could do without." Bailey took a big bite off the tip of her pizza.

Tane took a slice and leaned his back on the counter. He watched her as she washed down her pizza with the beer. She handed it to him, and he took a swig. It wasn't lost on him that her lips were just on the bottle. "So, you have one more year of high school. Any idea what you want to do once you graduate?"

"Oh, I already have my career planned out. I'm going to be a hairstylist."

"So, you plan to go to beauty school?" Bailey laughed, and Tane asked, "What? Isn't that what they call it?"

"Yeah, like fifty years ago. It's called cosmetology school, and I've already started. I do a half day at my high school and the other half at the career center. When I graduate, I will have my license to cut hair in the state of New York."

"Wow, I did not know that."

"Yes, so I could cut your hair so you can stop flipping it out of your eyes. If you want." Bailey took the beer Tane had placed on the counter and took a drink. "I have all my stuff in the car."

"Uh, you're still in school. How many haircuts have you given?"

"I cut my dad's hair all the time. I don't have enough hours to actually work on customers yet. But I have mannequin heads that I get graded on. I promise I won't leave you with an embarrassing haircut."

Tane gave it some thought and said, "Why not."

Bailey started clapping, "Yay, I get to do a young person for a change. I'll be right back." She put her half-eaten slice of pizza back in the box.

Tane liked seeing Bailey happy but wasn't so sure about the haircut. It did mean she would stay longer. He picked up the beer and took a swig. Maybe a little liquid courage. Tane finished off the bottle by the time Bailey returned.

Bailey put her stuff on the kitchen table and pulled out one of the chairs. "Sit here." She went to the sink and filled a spray bottle with water. Tane's hair had dried from his shower earlier. Bailey took her cape and put it around his neck.

Tane said, "So far, it looks professional." Bailey began wetting down his hair. After finishing the back, she moved around to do the same to the front of his hair. That's when Tane noticed her chest was at his eye level. That was until he had to quickly close them.

"Oops, sorry. I didn't mean to get it in your eyes."

"That's coming off your tip," Tane joked with her.

"Since the haircut is free, I don't expect much of a tip. I'm gaining experience."

Tane stopped her movements, "I would not expect you to do this for free. I'll pay you what I normally pay for a haircut."

Bailey leaned in to speak, "Tane, I...." Her face was close to his, she straightened and went back to cutting his hair. "You don't have to," and changed the subject, "So, you'll be off to college soon."

Tane closed his eyes and thought, *here we go.* "Yes, I'll be leaving in a month."

"So, what are you going to school for?"

"I'm going to become a priest."

Bailey stopped what she was doing to look at him. "For real?" She went back to cutting his hair. "I know your family always kidded about you becoming a priest, but I didn't realize you actually planned to do that." She said under her breath, "What a shame."

"Why do you say that?"

21

"Say what?"

"It's a shame. Giving yourself to God is never shameful."

Bailey didn't realize she said that loud enough for him to hear. "I think you're too cute to become a priest."

"Becoming a priest doesn't have anything to do with looks. It's about serving God."

Bailey kept moving as she said, "My family doesn't do the church thing. I know your family is big into that, with your uncle being a priest and all. How do you know you want to do that?"

"I've always seen myself becoming a priest."

"So, you never plan to have sex? I know that's a personal question, but you must be a virgin, right?"

Tane knew this would be tricky. "Not necessarily. In certain circumstances, men who have been married, and widowed have become priests."

"At least they knew what they were giving up. How can you make such a big decision without all the data? I guess what I'm saying is, you wouldn't invest in a company without knowing all the facts. If you never, let's say, kissed a girl as an example. How do you know you won't ever want to?"

"My uncle made it to the priesthood without ever kissing a girl. As far as him wanting to. He said he had feelings for someone, but she liked someone else. He went off to college, and that was the end of that. I feel I should be able to do the same."

"That might have been the path he was meant to take. But you are not your uncle." Bailey finished Tane's haircut and took the cape off. "Besides, kissing a girl is not a sin. I do know that."

"So, what are you suggesting?"

{3}

"What am **I** suggesting?" Bailey put her hand on her chest. "I just think you need to think about this, that's all."

"So, you aren't suggesting I kiss someone?"

"Oh, I am," she shook her head.

Tane got up from the chair and took her hand. She quickly put her scissors on the kitchen table as Tane pulled her into the living room. He started up the stairs, stopped short as if he had just remembered something, and then went to the couch instead. This time he didn't sit as far away from her as he could. No, he sat very close.

"Tane, what are you doing?"

"I'm going to kiss you."

That was the only warning she got before Tane's lips touched hers. He was stiff and uncomfortable. Bailey pulled back. "Tane, I don't think you want to kiss me."

"I do. I just don't know how."

Bailey never thought she'd be saying this, "How about I kiss you? Try to relax." She got up and sat in Tane's lap. Slowly, Bailey leaned in and pressed her lips to his. This time she ran her tongue across his bottom lip. Tane's mouth opened to her as their tongues touched and twirled around each other. Bailey's hands went into Tane's hair as she held him to her. Tane's hands came around her small waist and pulled her in close to his body.

Tane felt as if he was having an out-of-body experience. It was like he was dreaming but better because Bailey was in his arms. Sitting on his very hard penis. *Oh shit.*

The back door flew open, "Hey Tane, whose car is in the driveway?"

Tane jumped up, almost knocking Bailey to the floor. Tane whispered, "Sneak into the hall bathroom when I give you the all-clear." He went into the kitchen to see his brother Gabe and Faith standing there with a bag of laundry.

Faith looked around, "Who got a haircut?"

Tane tried to sound normal, "Hey, what are you guys doing here?"

Gabe looked down the hallway, "Whose here, Tane?"

"Bailey's here. She came to drop off some decorations for Julia's baby shower. Ray told her to bring them by."

Faith picked up the cutting shears off the table, "And she cut your hair?"

"I needed one, and she's in school to become a hairstylist. She asked if she could, and I said yes. No big deal."

Bailey crept as close to the hallway as she dared, waiting for the voices to move away from the kitchen.

Gabe asked, "So where is she? Oh, boy, she better not be upstairs." He rushed by Tane with Faith on his heels.

She said, "Gabe, let it go."

Tane followed Faith but didn't go up the stairs. He looked for Bailey but didn't see her.

Bailey rushed into the dining room just in time. She went through the kitchen and into the bathroom once she knew they were out of sight.

Tane caught sight of her and smiled. He yelled to his brother, "She's not up there, you ass. Bailey is in the bathroom down here."

Faith was the first one to come down. "I'm sorry, Tane."

"I didn't want to embarrass her. I should have known better that Gabe wouldn't care."

The bathroom door opened, and Bailey came out. Faith shook her head and yelled up the stairs, "Gabe, Bailey is right here. She came out of the bathroom."

Bailey looked at Faith, "I was cleaning the hair off my shirt."

Faith asked, "So you're going to school to be a cosmetologist?" They moved back into the kitchen. "I love to add some color to my hair. Maybe one time we can get together, and you can do my hair."

"I'd love to." Bailey picked up her sheers and shook out her cape.

Faith asked, "How did I not know this about you?"

"I guess we never really talked." Bailey looked over at Tane, "Thanks for letting me cut your hair."

Gabe came downstairs, "So… if she dropped off decorations, where are they? And Bro, you might want to pick up your dirty underwear off the bathroom floor."

Tane shook his head, "Bailey put them in Mom's sewing room like Ray told her to." Tane pulled his phone from his pocket, "Do you want me to call her to confirm?"

"No." Gabe spotted the pizza box and the beer sitting on the counter. "Who had a beer?" He picked up the empty bottle.

"Okay, Gabe, that's enough." Faith started pushing him towards the door. "You are not his father. Let's go. Sorry to bother you two. We'll be going now."

"We still need to do laundry."

"You lost your opportunity. We'll call before we come again," Faith closed the door behind them.

Tane said, "Aren't you glad you're an only child? I sure wish I was."

"Tane, about what happened in the other room." Bailey tried not to look at him as she folded her cape. "I'm not sure this is a good idea. I don't want to get hurt or feel like I'm being used, so you can sort out your feelings."

Tane hadn't thought about how this might hurt her. All he knew was he wanted to kiss her and much more. "I'm sorry. I didn't think about how this might make you feel." Tane rubbed the back of his neck, "I've just been thinking about you, and there you were, standing at my door."

"I should go." Tane stepped in her way.

"I don't want you to go." He crowded her against the wall, looking down at her. "Can I ask you a personal question?"

"I...ah, don't know."

"You don't have to answer if you don't want to." He looked down at her, "Have you already had, sex?"

Bailey pushed Tane back, "I don't think I want to answer that." She turned to face him, "I have one for you. Did you kiss me just because you knew I liked you, and it would be easy?"

Tane shook his head, "No. I kissed you because I wanted to know what it would feel like." He laughed to hide his discomfort, "I've thought about it a lot. Even dreamt about it and more. I prayed, hoping to get you out of my head. I feel as if God is testing me, and I'm failing miserably." Tane turned his back on her as he said, "I'm sorry. I shouldn't have involved you. I told myself to stay away from you."

"So, I guess we shouldn't be friends." Bailey looked at the floor, "I get it. I did like getting to know you. Good luck on your road to becoming a priest." Bailey walked to the front door and left.

Tane leaned his back against the wall. He tried to tell himself it was for the best. *She caught me off guard, a weak moment. I can do this. I just need to pray more.* Tane pushed off the wall to throw away the beer bottle and wrap up the pizza. In his head, he began reciting his penance as he went upstairs to his room and stopped short when he realized his sheets were in the washer. He couldn't catch an F-in break today. Tane went in search of sheets to put back on his bed. He gave up and went to sleep on the couch. Tane made sure all the doors were locked and flipped on the TV. He hoped it would stop him from dreaming. But now that he knew what it was like to kiss Bailey, he wasn't sure that would work.

Bailey made it home and threw herself across her bed. *What were you thinking kissing Tane? Oh, My God, I kissed him.* Bailey put her arm over her face, and Tane opening the door without a shirt, came to mind. He was so thin it made every muscle in his body show. *Hell, don't get me started on his chest hair or that happy trail. I*

can't believe Tane actually asked me if I was a virgin. I would have liked to say yes, but we all know that's a lie.

Bailey rolled over on her side, "It was too good to be true. Why would Tane want me? He's leaving for college, and I'm still in high school." Bailey sighed, "Well, you need to forget that kiss. It didn't mean anything. He's just trying to figure out what he wants." *And it ain't you. How do you know? He did say he thought about kissing me. Boys lie to get what they want. You learned that the hard way.* Bailey looked through her phone. It didn't take long before she was checking out Tane's social media page for like the millionth time. It was the only place that had pictures of him. Bailey sat up, "Maybe Faith would have some pictures of Tane on her page.

The problem was Bailey didn't know Faith's last name. So, she moved on to Gabe. Bailey didn't care for him. He went out of his way to be a jerk. The way he tried to embarrass Tane with the comment about his clothes being on the bathroom floor. It wasn't hard to find Gabe O'Shea's social media page, and there was Faith. Bailey sent a friend request and waited. It wasn't long before she accepted. Bailey smiled, "Yes, I'm in."

Her phone dinged. Faith had sent her a message. Faith: I'm sorry for busting in on you guys.

Bailey: No worries. We weren't doing anything but hanging out.

Faith: Gabe can be a dick sometimes. I'm sorry if he embarrassed you. I had a little talk with him on the way home.

Bailey: I'm fine. Like I said, we weren't doing anything. I mean, come on, Tane is becoming a priest. What did Gabe think we were doing anyway?

Faith: He's thinking along the lines of, if he was alone in the house, what he'd be doing. LOL

Bailey: Then I would think he'd give Tane a break and not bust his balls.

Faith: You would think. We should get together sometime. Maybe have lunch?

Bailey: I'd like that. I don't really fit in with the O'Shea's. I'm just a stand-in for all the weddings to help even out all the boys in the family.

Faith: Everyone is matched up except Tane.

Bailey: Yep, and I think Tane resents the fact that everyone keeps pairing us up. He talked to me more tonight than I've ever heard him speak. I think he was so talkative because he was alone in the house, and we were one-on-one.

Faith: Bailey, be careful. The O'Shea's have a way of sucking you in.

Bailey: I've been around a few years now and still haven't been sucked in. I think I'm safe.

The conversation hit a lull, and Faith didn't write back. Bailey threw her phone on her bed and went back to thinking about Tane without his shirt.

Tane couldn't get comfortable on the couch. He flipped the covers back and got up. If he couldn't sleep, he might as well do something instead of just lying there. After collecting his clothes off the bathroom floor, he started a load of laundry. Tane got out the ice cream and dished out a big, heaping spoonful. He was looking through his phone at the news and weather. When he thought, *why haven't I looked her up on social media. She admitted to looking at mine.*

Tane hit the app and went in search of Bailey's page. *What if she has pictures with other guys on there? Cross that bridge when we get to it. What if I find out things about her that I don't like? Good, it will help your cause.* It didn't take long to find Bailey's page. Tane took a deep breath and started flipping through her pictures. She was so damn cute. He checked her out first and then took in what was in the background. She saw his bedroom, but he had no clue what hers looked like. He didn't even know where she lived.

After he went through all her pictures, he checked out her profile. Bailey had her phone number, and Tane put it in his phone. He sat at the kitchen table debating whether or not to call her. He could say he was calling because she never got her tip, and he wanted to send her money. Before he could talk himself out of it, he hit call. Bailey's voice said, "Hi, it's Bailey. You know what to do."

Tane said, "Hi, it's Tane. I know it's late, but I figured you'd be awake. I never gave you the tip I promised you. I wanted to send it to you, but I don't have your email. Call me back...if you want." Tane quickly hung up. He put his phone on the table. "That was stupid. She will think I like her." *You do, so don't even try to deny it.*

It wasn't long before he got a text from Bailey.

Bailey: I told you that wasn't necessary but thank you.

Tane: You gave me a great haircut, and I want to show you I appreciate it.

Bailey: That's sweet, but I can't accept it.

Tane: Come on, Bailey. Just give me your email and let me do this.

Bailey: How did you get my number?

Tane: I looked you up on social media. Cute pictures, by the way.

Bailey: Tane, what are you doing? You can't be flirting with me if you are becoming a priest. Besides, you don't like me, remember?

Tane: What if I say I changed my mind?

Bailey: About becoming a priest or liking me?

Tane put his feet up on the bench on the other side of the table as he thought about what to say next. Tane: I'm confused because I liked kissing you. I think we had fun until we were interrupted.

Bailey: I think you're taking advantage of me because you know I like you.

Tane: I'm not.

Bailey: So, what would have happened if your brother and Faith hadn't come?

Tane: I don't know.

Bailey: I don't think it's a good idea for us to be alone if you still plan to become a priest.

Tane: Why? You don't think I can control myself?

Bailey: I don't think you should be tempting fate. I would hate to be the one that pulls you away from your path.

Tane: Do you think you can?

Bailey: If you keep this up, you just might find out. Good night, Tane.

Tane threw his phone on the table. His bowl of ice cream was now melted. "Why am I doing this to myself? I say I will stay away from her, and then I'm texting her. On the one hand, you know she's no good for you, and on the other, you can't seem to stay away from her." Tane got up and rinsed his bowl, letting the melted ice cream go down the drain. "You need to get a grip, man." The washing machine signaled it was done. Tane went to put the clothes into the dryer. He sat his sneakers on top to air dry.

Tane picked up his phone and sent Bailey a friend request. He didn't think she would accept it right away, but it was worth a try. Tane decided he wasn't ready to sleep. He needed to clean up the hair on the kitchen floor. Tane got out the vacuum cleaner. Before he knew it, he was cleaning the entire bottom floor of the house. Once he was done, he needed another shower. Tane sat on the couch. "Wow, that was a lot of work. I never realized how much goes into keeping this house clean." He wiped the sweat from his face. His mother kept a spotless house. Tane thought how he was the last one to live at home full time and now he was getting ready to go off to college. His parents didn't need such a big house anymore.

Tane looked into the dining room where his father and brothers ripped out the wall to make it bigger. That room needed to be larger. He was sure if his family kept growing, he'd get pushed out of the dining room and would be eating in the kitchen. These days they have more highchairs around the table. With Bryant and Macy's two, and Ray and Jon's twins. Soon Mack and Julia would have a kid, too. Tane put his feet up on the coffee table. "Who will be next? Grace, maybe? Of course, Paul and Lauren still have to get married first. Then there's Gabe and Faith who are engaged and Patrick and Shana. I give Ava and Daniel plenty of time. I'm sure Ava will want to finish school first."

What about you? Who will be sitting at the table with you?

Tane put his feet down and sat up. "No one will be at the table with me. I most likely won't even be in a church anywhere near here once I become a priest." Tane hadn't thought about how he'd be away from his family, and his days at Sunday dinners were numbered. He always felt having such a big family was a pain in the butt, but now the thought of not having them made him feel a little lost. He was the youngest. The one pulling up the rear.

Tane closed his eyes and thought about how his life would be as a priest. He would be doing Mass on Sundays. Just like his uncle did. His uncle wasn't at every Sunday dinner. He was serving the Lord. "That's what I want too."

Are you one hundred percent sure?

"I was, until." Tane opened his eyes, and he was sitting in the same spot he had Baily sitting on his lap, kissing her. "Maybe not so sure." He knew it was temptation. It went back as far as Adam and Eve. Did he want a taste of the forbidden fruit? "The way Baily kissed me and how I kissed her back. I would say yes."

Try saying your penance.

"Yeah, because that worked so well the last time." Tane got up and turned out all the lights. He looked at his phone to see Bailey accepted his friend request.

Her words came back to him, "*How can you make such a big decision without all the data? I guess what I'm saying is, you wouldn't invest in a company without knowing all the facts. If you never, let's say, kissed a girl as an example. How do you know you won't ever want to?*"

He knew the answer to that question, he did want to, and that was the problem.

{4}

Tane woke on the couch again. He took a deep breath because he didn't dream of Bailey, which was a good sign. He fell asleep saying the prayers his uncle gave him for penance. It was a new day, and he had no plans to see or talk to Bailey. Maybe if he stayed clear of her his thoughts of her would pass. *Not likely.*

He put his feet on the floor and sat up. Tane wiped his face with his hands. Today was day three of his parents being gone. He didn't have to work, so what did he want to do? He needed to mow the front lawn before it got too high. *Yeah, you know what happened the last time you mowed the lawn.* "How could I forget? It was yesterday."

It was also the day you had your lips on...

"Shut up. We aren't thinking about that."

Okay, if you say so.

"I do," Tane shook his head. He'd only been alone for two days and he was not only talking to himself but answering himself too. "I can do anything I want. Now, what do I want to do?" He got off the couch to get something to eat. He'd start there.

Tane went into the kitchen to get a bowl of cereal. His phone was sitting on the table. Tane sat down, glancing through it, and tried not to click on social media because he knew where that would lead. Although he did owe her a tip for cutting his hair. *How can I get it to her? She wouldn't give you her email address, so what now.* "I should just let it go."

But you know you don't want to do that. He clicked on the social media app and went right to her page. This time he didn't look through her posts but the about her section. "Bingo, she has where she works. I can go by there and see if she's working. Nothing too stalkish about showing up at her job. I love ice cream, especially thirty-one flavors."

Now that he had a plan, Tane put the dryer on to fluff up his clothes while he took a shower. That was another thing that wouldn't have happened if his mother had been around.

Bailey did her best to concentrate on what flavors of ice cream her customer asked for. They liked to give her fifteen different flavors and sizes all at once. This one gets sprinkles that one gets hot sauce. This one in a cup that one in a cone. She would do one or two at a time and then ask again what else they wanted. Bailey liked to watch them try to figure out what they still needed. She glanced up to speak to her customer and spotted Tane standing in line.

"I…I'm sorry what else did you say?"

"We want a large waffle cone with Double Fudge, a small cone with Peanut Butter 'n Chocolate with sprinkles, and a…"

Bailey held up her finger. "Hold that thought." She grabbed the waffle cone and began scooping out the ice cream.

The other girl Bailey was working with said, "I'll take the next customer in line."

Tane let the person behind him go. He waited for Bailey to be free. "Tane what are you doing here?"

"I came to get some ice cream." He leaned in over the counter, and said quietly, "I still owe you a tip from yesterday."

Bailey looked at the other girl, who was watching them. She said in the same hushed tone, "I told you that wasn't necessary. What can I get for you, Sir?"

"What's your favorite flavor?"

"I," Bailey looked down at all the ice cream tubs. "I like Mint Chocolate Chip. What can I get you?"

"I'll have a large Mint Chocolate Chip, and can I have that dipped in chocolate?"

"Do you want hot fudge or the one that hardens?"

Tane smiled, "The second one." He watched as she scooped out his ice cream, "When do you get off?"

Bailey looked over at her co-worker, then quietly said, "I'm done at three."

"Do you get a break? Can you sit with me?"

"Tane."

Her co-worker who was obviously listening to their conversation said, "Yes, she can sit with you. I'll take care of the customers while she takes her break."

Tane paid for his ice cream, and they went to sit at a table. "Tane what are you doing here? How did you even know where I worked?"

"Does it matter how I found you? You could have avoided all this if you just gave me your email address." Tane took a bite from his ice cream.

Bailey rolled her eyes, "Fine, if you must know." She got up and grabbed the pen by the register. "Give me your hand," when Tane held it out she wrote her email on it. "Now you have my email address. Is there anything else you want?"

"Yeah, I want us to hang out after you get off of work."

"Tane why are you doing this?"

"I'm gathering my data." He pulled off a slab of chocolate from his cone and stuck it in his mouth.

Bailey looked confused, "Your what?"

"You know, my data before investing in my future. You said I should know all the facts before I decide."

"I didn't mean… with me."

"Why not you? I liked kissing you and I'm sure…"

Bailey put up her hand, "Stop right there. Just because I didn't answer your question about having sex. Doesn't mean I will with you."

"I didn't say anything about sex." Tane licked the green ice cream running down his cone.

"What exactly do you want from me?"

"I want to go on a few dates and see how it feels."

Bailey shook her head, no. "Tane, I have feelings you know. Just because you think I like you doesn't mean I want to be your trial run."

"I'm sorry. I didn't mean to make it sound that way. I never had anyone I wanted to spend time with before." Tane shrugged, "I liked hanging out with you. I don't know how that will affect my becoming a priest, but I think I owe it to myself to be sure. It's not a sin to date. What do you say?"

"What happens when things get carried away like they did the other night? I don't think this is a good idea."

"So, you think things will go beyond kissing?"

"I'd bet on it."

Tane smiled, "Really, you'd bet on it?"

"I've never seen this side of you. Normally, you don't say two words to me and now you want to date. I don't get you."

"So, you get off at three?"

"Why?"

"Because I want to take you out, silly." Tane swiped some ice cream on his finger and tapped her nose.

Bailey quickly grabbed a napkin and wiped it away. She looked at her co-worker, and said under her breath, "Stop that. I have to work here you know."

Tane took another swipe and held it out, "Say yes."

Bailey leaned forward and sucked the ice cream off Tane's finger. "Fine. Now you need to go." She went to get up and Tane stopped her.

"I need your address to pick you up."

"I can come by your house."

"Nope, this is a date. I pick you up and take you home. Be sure to wear a hat, and dress casual."

"Where we going?"

"It's a surprise."

"I don't like surprises. So, just tell me."

"Not a chance. Be ready by six."

"I think I liked you better when you weren't a talker. You're a little bossy."

Tane laughed, "You have met my family, right?"

"Yeah, but you were the quiet one."

Tane pulled a napkin out of the dispenser and slid it across the table. "I need your address."

Bailey rolled her eyes. She wrote on the napkin and handed it back to him. "I'll be ready for whatever you have in mind." Bailey saw Tane's expression and said, "I mean the date." He leaned in kissed her and walked out.

Bailey went behind the counter. Her co-worker stood there looking at her. "So, are you going to tell me who that tall glass of water was?"

Bailey laughed, "I told you about Tane. He's the one that I always get paired with for the O'Shea weddings."

"You mean the one that didn't like you? Because he seemed pretty into you."

A customer came into the store saving Bailey from explaining what was happening between her and Tane. Once she finished her shift, Bailey went home to get ready for her date.

Tane rushed to the box office. He knew if he got tickets, they would be nosebleeds, but it was a last-minute decision. Once Tane had his tickets in hand, he went home to get ready for his first date ever. After he showered, Tane put on some of the body spray his mother gave him for Christmas that he never bothered to use. He just didn't want to overdo it like some guys did. Tane hated when you'd walk by someone, and you could smell them from five feet away. It was just as bad as an old lady wearing too much perfume.

Tane threw on his favorite pair of jeans and a T-shirt. He took his baseball cap into the bathroom so he could put it on in the mirror. It occurred to him that he'd never cared how it looked on his head before. Tane adjusted his hair, so it wasn't sticking up. He looked at his shirt, deciding he didn't like it. Tane left the bathroom and went into his sister's room where they had a full-length mirror. He turned to look at his jeans. His butt looked saggy. They were his favorite pants because they were comfortable not for how they looked. He pulled off his hat and then his shirt, and next went his jeans.

After changing two or three times, Tane was ready to go. He made sure he had the tickets, keys to get back into the house, his wallet, and some cash. Tane didn't plan to drive his mother's car because it was easier to take the bus to the subway. He left in plenty of time to get to Bailey's place. Tane moved through the city with ease, and he wasn't surprised to see Bailey lived in a brownstone. He looked at the tall building and went up the stairs to ring the bell. A dark-haired woman answered the door. "Can I help you?"

"Yes, I'm Tane O'Shea and I'm here to pick up Bailey." The woman stepped aside to let him in.

"I will tell her you're here."

Bailey started down the stairs, "That won't be necessary, Louisa. Come on Tane."

Tane looked at the woman, and when she didn't say anything, he followed Bailey up the stairs. Apparently, Bailey's parents had money. Tane looked around as he went up the two flights of stairs. "Nice place you have here."

"Don't be impressed. My parents are never around because they have to pay for this place. I'd much rather have your house where it feels warm. This place is cold and uninviting." Bailey walked into her room.

Tane looked around and was amazed at the size of her space. It wasn't as big as his sister's room but all three of them shared that room at one point. His bedroom was probably the size of her closet. His parents most likely converted the small space into his bedroom because they were running out of room.

"Have a seat. I'm going to change. I wasn't sure what to wear so, I figured I'd see what you had on first."

Tane looked around and sat on her bed. He felt uncomfortable as he folded his hands in between his knees. Bailey went into the bathroom to change but didn't close the door all the way. "So, are you going to tell me where we're going?"

"No," he could see her through the crack in the door. Bailey pulled her shirt over her head and Tane's breathing accelerated. Next, she took off her pants. Bailey wore a light pink bra and thong. Tane's dick responded appropriately, and he readjusted his crotch.

"I don't know what the big deal is." Bailey moved out of view and Tane wasn't sure if that was a good thing. The bathroom door opened, and she came out fully dressed, with her hair in two little braids. Bailey moved to her closet again to pull out a baseball cap and leaned over so she could look in her vanity mirror as she put the hat on her head.

Tane's eyes were glued to her sweet ass, now that he knew what was under her jeans. She turned and his eyes snapped up to her face. "It's…what did you say?" He lost his train of thought.

"I didn't say anything. I asked what the big deal was."

"Oh, right. It's not a big deal. I just want you to be surprised that's all." Tane stood and stepped up to her. He gave her braids a little tug. "You look cute with your hair like this."

Bailey looked up at Tane. He was acting so differently towards her, warm and kind. Normally, he'd either ignore her altogether or just mumble something.

"Why are you looking at me like that?"

"I'm trying to figure you out. One day you don't want to speak to me and all I get is a few mumbled words and then you're holding my hair telling me I look cute."

"It's not hard to understand. I didn't want to like you before or to get to know you. I didn't want to think about you at all. But I can't help it."

"Tane, you are becoming a priest. I don't want to get hurt. You know I like you, and I think you're…" He kissed her words away. She pulled back, "I think we should be friends like you said."

He took her hand, "Let's go."

Bailey let Tane lead her out of her room. She had a bad feeling about this thing with him. He would get what he wanted and leave her broken. Bailey was surprised when they walked out the door and started moving down the sidewalk. She asked, "Where's your car?"

"I didn't bring it. We're riding the subway."

Bailey stopped walking, "The subway?"

Tane turned to face her, "Yes, this way we don't need to worry about parking. The subway will drop us off right outside the stad…where we're going."

Bailey didn't say anything, and they walked in silence. She decided no matter how cute or how much she'd like to have Tane as her boyfriend, she needed to protect her heart. Have fun and walk away, once he went off to college, she'd move on. The thought that he'd end things once his parents came home from their cruise crossed her mind. He was being nice to her because no one knew about them. Well, Faith and Gabe knew she was over at his house, but they didn't know he wanted to…What did he want? "Tane, can I ask you a question?" They moved down into the subway."

"Sure, ask me anything."

"What do you want from me?"

Tane looked down the tracks, "What do you mean?"

"I mean, you kiss me like I'm your girlfriend. You tell me kissing isn't a sin. You still plan to be a priest so what are you doing with me? Am I just someone easy to experiment on? What are we doing?"

Tane faced her, "Bailey, it's called dating. I'm not sure what my future plans are. If you asked me a few months ago, I would have told you I knew what I wanted. But I'm not so sure anymore. I'm not with you because you're easy. I like you."

"So, when your parents get back will we still be," Bailey made air quotes, "Dating?" Because it feels like you're trying to keep what we're doing a secret."

"I'm not trying to hide anything. Am I trying to avoid all the crap my family will give me about this? I guess I am."

"So, if I talked to Faith, would you want me to mention we went on a date or keep it to myself?"

"Faith isn't the problem. It's Gabe that would be a dick about it. Look, I don't want you to think I'm trying to hide what we're doing. I'm not ashamed to be seen with you. I wouldn't care if Ava or Grace knew. Ray can be a little over the top, but it's the guys that I don't want to know. I don't want them saying anything about you."

"You think they'd say something bad about me? Mack is married to my aunt. I'm his niece."

"Okay, Mack wouldn't say anything about you, but I'm sure he'd say something about not becoming a priest. They wouldn't be saying it to be mean to you but say things to get at me."

"Wow, I thought your family was nice."

"They are, but…"

"You still didn't answer my question about where this is going."

The train pulled into the station and that was the end of their conversation. Tane held her hand as they rode the train to their stop. They got up and went up to the street. They were right outside of Citi Field. Tane pulled out his wallet and handed Bailey a ticket.

"Were going to a baseball game?"

"Yep." They went through the gate and made their way to the upper deck. "We won't be catching any home runs from up here, but it was the best I could do on such short notice."

"I didn't know you liked baseball."

"There's a lot of things you don't know about me. This is all general admission. So, we can sit anywhere you want."

"Let's sit as close as we can."

"That's where all the people are. If we sit a little higher, we can be away from everyone else."

"You're such an introvert." Tane just smiled at her, and she felt her heart skip a beat.

{5}

Before the game started, Tane offered to get Bailey something to eat and drink. He was surprised by what she wanted. Tane would have pegged her for a salad kind of girl. "I'll be right back," he said.

Tane made his way to the concession area and got in line. He thought to himself, *why didn't we get all this before we went to our seats? Because you've never been on a date before and only had yourself to think about.*

Once Tane made it to the front of the line, he ordered two dogs all the way, fries, popcorn, and two drinks. The guy was nice enough to give him a carrier for the food and drinks. Tane made his way back to where Bailey sat. He noticed she had lifted the armrest that had been in between them. She took the drinks, putting them in the cup holder. Tane handed her a hotdog and left the fries in the container, putting it in between them, so they both could reach them.

Tane watched as Bailey opened her hotdog and took a big bite. She didn't seem to care that he was looking at her. He opened his and began eating. Bailey had some chilly on her face. Tane took a napkin to wipe it away. She looked up at him and said, "Thank you."

"I thought about kissing it away, but I thought you might not like that."

Bailey smiled, "You could have done that. We are on a date after all."

"Good to know."

It wasn't long before the baseball game started, and Tane and Bailey polished off the fries and moved on to the popcorn. He was impressed by what she ate. Bailey put away just as much food as he did. He wondered how she stayed so skinny. Tane eased his arm around her shoulder, and she relaxed into his side. They had the tub of popcorn sitting on Bailey's lap. Tane liked the way it felt to have her pressed to his side.

The game wasn't very exciting. There wasn't even a run in the top of the fifth inning. Tane decided to make it more interesting. He tilted her head to face his and kissed her. Bailey responded the way he'd hoped she would. By the time the seventh inning stretch came, Tane was ready to take Bailey back to his house. Just then, Mr. Met, the team's mascot, started moving toward them.

Tane said, "Uh-oh. I think he's coming this way."

Bailey agreed, "Yep, he sure is."

Mr. Met moved into the aisle before theirs and reached out for Bailey's hand. She took it and Mr. Met led her to the flat part of the stairs and began to dance with Bailey. Tane stood in disbelief. He looked up at the big jumbotron and sure enough, he saw Mr. Met and Bailey dancing. Tane wanted to reclaim his date, but he didn't want to make a scene.

It wasn't long before Mr. Met was returning Bailey to her seat. This time, the Mets mascot walked into the row behind as he led Bailey back into the row that Tane sat in. Once Bailey sat down, Mr. Met pointed to them.

Tane saw they were still on the jumbotron, but now it was the kiss cam. He leaned in and kissed Bailey. A nice long kiss, and the crowd went wild. Once they broke the kiss, Tane and Bailey waved to the crowd. After they were no longer on the screen, Tane leaned into Bailey and said, "Are you ready to get out of here?"

"Let's go."

Tane held her hand as they made their way out of the stadium. She asked, "Are you taking me home, or we doing something else?"

"I thought we could go back to my house."

"Tane, I'm not sure that's a good idea."

"Why? Do you think something is going to happen?"

"I just think when we're out in public, it's safer."

"What if I promise nothing more than a kiss will happen. Would you be okay with that?"

"I guess."

They got on the subway and headed in the direction of his house. Bailey felt butterflies in her stomach. *Just don't let things get out of hand,* she told herself. *But what if he wants to do more? Do I have the willpower to stop Tane?*

Tane leaned in to speak into her ear, "Nothing's going to happen. Well, nothing I'll have to go to confession for."

"Okay," Bailey tried to relax.

Tane stood when they got to their stop, and Bailey followed him off the subway. They moved to the bus stop. As they waited Tane asked, "Are you nervous to be alone with me?"

"I guess I am."

"Why?"

"Tane, you know I like you, but I don't want to be the reason you change your mind about what you want to do with your life."

"I don't understand you. On one hand, you tell me to gather all the information to make an informed decision, and yet, you don't want to be the one to show me what I'd be missing."

"I'm not your test subject."

"So, what are you telling me? You want me to find someone else to show me?"

"Ah, I didn't say that. But I don't want to fall for you and then you decide to become a priest and leave me with a broken heart."

"I don't want that either. Bailey, I'm confused right now. I always wanted to become a priest, to give myself to the Lord. But then I started dreaming about you and something changed. It began with me wanting to know what it would feel like kissing you. Then how you'd feel in my arms. There's more but I don't think it's appropriate for me to tell you. I can't seem to get you out of my mind. I went to confession, and prayed over it, but every time I close my eyes, you're there."

"So, you dream about me? Like sex dreams?"

Tane looked down at Bailey's tiny stature and would love to get his hands on her body. "I know things I shouldn't, like the color of the bra and panties you're wearing right now."

Bailey's mouth fell open, "How do you know that?"

"I could see you changing through the crack in the bathroom door. I should have said something, but I wanted to watch."

Bailey punched Tane in the arm, "You freaking peeping Tom. I thought I had the door closed enough. I didn't close it all the way so I could still talk to you, not so you could get your thrills."

Tane leaned in to speak in Bailey's ear, "You are the first girl I've ever seen like that, and I'd like to see more, but I know that would be pushing things."

Bailey shook her head, "Wow, I'm not sure if I should take that as a compliment or if it makes me feel like a slut."

"Bailey, I never meant for...," the bus pulled up and that was the end of their conversation. They had to stand and Tane pulled her in close to his body. He took in the smell of her shampoo, and somehow it turned him on. Tane thought about how Bailey had put her hair in braids. He knew he'd seen her hair like that before but couldn't remember when. Then it hit him. Bailey wore her hair like that in his dream. The dream where he pinned her against the wall outside the pub, and he had his hands all over her body.

Tane went rigid and Bailey looked up at him as if she knew something was wrong. She asked, "Tane, what's wrong?"

He leaned down to speak into her ear, "I just thought of something. It's nothing."

Bailey glanced up into his eyes gauging the truth of his words. "If it's nothing, why did your entire body go stiff?"

"I'll tell you once we get off the bus." Tane didn't want to explain to Bailey about his dream or how he pretty much mauled her in his fantasy, but he couldn't lie to her. He'd have to find a way to tell her without making it sound like he was a complete jerk, or she was a slut.

Their stop came and Tane led Bailey off the bus. He was glad when she didn't ask what happened on the bus, but he knew she hadn't forgotten about it. Tane pulled out his keys and unlocked the door. They took off their shoes and went into the kitchen. That's when Bailey asked, "Are you going to tell me why you got all weird on the bus?"

"It's a little embarrassing. I don't want to tell you where you can see my face."

Bailey looked surprised, "You don't want me to see your face? Tane, what's going on?"

50

Tane took her hand and led her to the stairs. Bailey stopped moving and held her ground, "Tane, why are you taking me upstairs?"

"I want to tell you but…I promise nothing's going to happen." Bailey let him take her to his room. Tane lifted her up on his bed. He took off their hats and closed the door. The room was dark, and he said, "Lay down next to me."

"Tane, why are you acting so weird? You're scaring me."

Once he had her next to him, he began to tell Bailey what was going on in his head, "I told you how I've dreamt about you, right?"

"Yes," Bailey answered and waited for Tane to say more.

"I'm sorry, I don't want you to feel as if I don't respect you, because I do."

"Okay."

"The dreams were very sexual in nature."

"I figured that was the case."

"You did?"

"Tane, everyone has subconscious thoughts and dreams. We can't control what our mind is thinking when we're asleep."

"I was very disturbed by how raw and how much I wanted to touch every inch of your body. How I did touch you."

"Tane, we all do that. The other day, when you came to the door with no shirt on, that sent my mind to places, I don't want to say."

"See, that's what I'm talking about. I realized you wore your hair in those two little braids in one of my very explicit dreams and well, you can imagine how my body reacted. I find this embarrassing. I'm not supposed to be having thoughts like this. I never did before and now you seem to be taking up an awful lot of space in my head. I

51

want to do things I never even considered doing before. I've tried to get you out of my head. I prayed about it. I've talked to my Uncle Joe."

Bailey's voice got loud, "You told your uncle about me?"

"I never mentioned your name. Not that I think he doesn't know it's you. I'm starting to think God wants me to go down a different path."

"Do you really think, God would make you have sex dreams about me, to get you to not become a priest? I find that hard to believe. Not that I follow any religion."

Tane turned to face Bailey and put his hand up to support his head. "I think God would test my own free will. He would show me what I'd be giving up for him, and he'd want me to choose him freely."

Bailey asked, "So, that brings us back to, what are we doing in your bed?"

"It was the only place I could think of that it'd be dark. I didn't want to see the look in your eyes when I told you about my dreams and what I did to you, or want to do to you."

Bailey now turned to face Tane, "What do you want to do to me?"

"I'm not sure you want to know the things I've thought about."

"Why don't you tell me. We aren't doing anything but talking, right?"

"Do you think that's a good idea?"

"You could suffer alone, or we could talk about it. Why don't you tell me about the dream where I have my hair in braids?"

"You promise not to look at me differently if I tell you?"

"How about I tell you one of mine?"

52

"You would do that? Tell me about your dreams?"

"They're more like short little blips, daydreams. Let's take when you opened the door with no shirt on and your pants hung low on your hips. I didn't get to fantasize about what I was seeing because you rudely asked me what I was doing there. I had to gather my thoughts and not let the fact that you were standing in front of me half-naked look like it affected me. But once you invited me to stay and went to take your shower. I did think about every inch of your body that I could see."

"Did you think about touching me?"

"Um, kinda."

"Kinda?"

"Well, I thought about your chest hair and how it would feel to run my fingers through it and your happy trail."

"My happy trail?"

"Oh, I forgot you're a virgin. A "happy trail" is the hair that grows from your belly button to…well you know." Bailey paused and went on, "I noticed that you have that deep V in your hips. It's like pointing to your…"

"I get it. Is that all the touching you thought about?"

"Girls are emotional."

"Don't I know it?"

"What I mean is, men are physical. Women fantasize more about a sensual touch whereas men it's about the physical, or as you put it raw. Your turn."

"Where do you get all this stuff?"

"I took a few psych classes. It's true. Think about it. I'm thinking about running my fingers through your chest hair and I bet you're thinking about sinking your cock in me."

"Something like that. There was a lot of touching too, and kissing. It wasn't just the act."

"You mean sex?"

"Well, yes. I don't know how you can be so matter of fact about this. Here I'm thinking about touching you and…"

"Having sex with me."

"And you act like it's no big deal."

"Tane, you are a normal male. Men think about sex all the time. It's a wonder they can get anything else done. I think they say men think about it every three or four seconds. You've never thought about sex before you thought about having it with me?"

"Call me a late bloomer, no. I had a plan and knew what my future held. Now, you come along and side-swiped me. I'm not sure of anything anymore."

"Hey, I didn't do anything but show up at your door with the decorations your sister told me to leave in your mother's sewing room."

Tane sighed, "I didn't mean it to sound like that. I was thinking about you before you showed up here. That's why I was mad when I opened the door because I was trying to stop thinking about you. I decided I owe it to myself and God to be sure the choice I'm making is the right one."

"So, you think laying in your bed talking about how we feel sexually about each other is a way to decide?"

"I don't know, but if I'm truthful. I like spending time with you." Tane's hand went to her head as he leaned in and found her lips in the dark. Bailey kissed him back as their tongues twisted around each other. She tangled her hands in his hair. Tane moved his hand down her back, pulling her closer to him. He shifted her leg over his as he rolled on top of her. Tane moved his hands to the bottom of her shirt and touched the skin on her ribcage, he continued to glide up to the bottom of her bra.

Bailey broke the kiss, "Tane what are you doing?"

"What feels right," he went back to kissing her. Tane's body was aligned with hers. He wanted her.

Bailey could feel Tane's hard-on, "Wait. I don't think this is a good idea. You aren't putting enough thought into this."

"That's all I've been doing is thinking about this. I want to touch you, know how you feel, your skin, your body."

"I'm afraid."

Her words got Tane's attention, "Afraid…of what…me?"

"Once we take this step, you'll walk away." Tane put his head down on the pillow next to her head. She could hear him breathing. "I'm sorry. I don't think you know what this means. Once we cross this line there's no going back. You can't take it back. Tane, if you choose not to become a priest and want to have a physical relationship with someone, it should be with someone you love, not…me." It broke Bailey's heart to say what she did but it was true. Tane didn't love her, he just knew she would most likely give him what he wanted. "I should go." When she pushed Tane, he rolled off of her. He hadn't said a word and Bailey could feel the tears beginning to fill her eyes.

"I should take you home."

"No, I can get home on my own." She quickly jumped off his bed and rushed down the stairs. She didn't want him to see her falling apart. Bailey grabbed her shoes and went out the door. She slipped them on as she moved down the street.

Tane stayed there for a few seconds with his arm over his face before he went after Bailey. He ran down the stairs and out the front door, not bothering with shoes. Tane yelled, "Bailey stop!"

Once Bailey heard him calling her name she began to run. There was no way she wanted Tane to catch her. The tears were streaming down her face.

Bailey was no match for him. He had long legs and caught up to her. "Bailey, wait."

"Go away Tane." She wouldn't look at him.

"No," Tane held onto her shoulders and tried to get her to look at him. She fought him and for such a small person Bailey put up a mighty damn good fight. "Stop!" Finally, he just swooped her over his shoulder. Tane carried her back to his house. He made a mess out of this and needed to fix it.

"I demand you put me down right now." Bailey pounded on Tane's back.

"Not until we talk."

"I don't want to talk to you. I said everything I wanted to say in your bedroom."

Tane waved to people who looked at them strangely, "Good evening."

"Tane!"

"Bailey."

{6}

Tane didn't stop moving until he sat Bailey down on his bed. They were right back where they started. "I made a mess out of this and I'm sorry. But you running away and us not talking for the next five days isn't going to fix this."

Bailey sat there with a blank expression on her face. Her lips were tightly pressed together. She had no plans to say a word.

Tane walked back and forth in his tiny room. "I should have never tried to push myself on you. I get that. Like you said I'm new at this."

"A virgin."

"Yes, we know that. I didn't have normal urges at the age of thirteen. I never wanted to experiment with anyone or touch anyone before you. Do I love you? I don't know because I've never dated or looked at someone and felt anything, until you that is." Tane stopped walking to look at Bailey, really look at her. "Do you know what I see when I look at you?"

"Someone that's easy."

Tane shook his head, "Not at all. I don't understand you. You'd think because I have three sisters, I would have a better understanding of the female world."

"I'm not your sister."

"Oh, don't I know it? You are someone completely different from anyone I know. You have turned my world upside down. You have this way of making me…want something I've never wanted before. Never thought about, never considered before."

"I stopped thinking about you and showed up to drop off…"

"Party decorations, I know." Tane pointed at her, "When did you stop thinking about me? Because I think that's when you turned on the switch."

"What are you talking about?" Bailey's plan of not talking went out the window. "I didn't turn on any switch. You made it clear you had no interest in me, so I decided to move on."

"When you were in the pub in the back room. Is that when you started to move on?"

"Tane, you are talking crazy. You yelled at me at your brother's wedding. I licked my wounds and decided to stop chasing you. I wasn't looking at you anymore. You didn't want me. A girl knows when to move on."

"Ah-ha, that's it! I noticed you didn't even look at me in the pub. You even rushed by me without a word."

"So? That's what you wanted."

"That's what, I thought, I wanted. But then I got thinking and the more I thought about you moving on, I didn't like it. Then you started showing up in my dreams." Tane started moving again and he was talking as if to himself. "Dreams, like I've never had before. Wet dreams. I tried to get you out of my head, but every time I turned around there you were. I tried to say prayers to get the thoughts of you out of my head and then you ring the doorbell, and nothing has been the same since."

Bailey watched Tane move from one side of his room to the other. "You're experiencing infatuation. Because I liked you and then stopped paying you the attention you craved. You think you like me because, in reality, you just liked me liking you." Tane stopped walking and he shook his head.

"But what about the dreams, the sexual stuff?"

"It's probably lust, something you've never felt before, and you're associating it with infatuation." Bailey was talking Tane right out of liking her. "The lust is strong because it didn't start until just recently. For most young boys it starts as you go through puberty and the more you have it, you start to understand the feelings."

"So, what do I do about them? How do I control them?"

"Tane, you have to suffer through them like everyone else in the human race. In time they will pass, and you'll be thanking me that we didn't…."

Tane stepped between her legs and looked into her eyes, "I'm sorry. I may not understand what my body is going through, but I know my feelings for you aren't just in my head. I still want to spend time with you. Would you like to go to church with me tomorrow?"

"Um, won't all your family be at church?"

Tane smiled, "Remember, my parents are out of town. I doubt anyone will show up and so what if they do."

Bailey's heart melted when he smiled at her, "I guess going to church is a safe place to be together."

Tane leaned in and kissed her. He didn't push for more, just a quick peck on the lips. "Let's get something to eat and watch a movie, what do you say?"

The drama passed and Bailey was going to stay clear of getting herself into that situation again. After they went to church, she would not answer Tane's calls. She needed to let him get his feelings in check along with her own. Tane went into the kitchen to heat up some of the leftover pizza from the other day and she was to find a movie to watch. After picking what they'd watch, Bailey went into the bathroom and looked at herself in the mirror. Her mascara made dark circles around her eyes from when she cried. Bailey attempted to fix it as she thought about how Tane had seen her like this. She wet her finger and glided it under each eye to remove the makeup. There wasn't much she could do about the rest except wash it all off. Bailey grabbed a washcloth and did just that. It didn't matter if she only looked like a twelve-year-old without any makeup.

Tane was sitting on the couch and the pizza on the cocktail table when Bailey came out. "I don't see your mother approving of eating in here, much less the pizza on her table." Bailey sat next to him.

"There's a lot of things I've done this week that my mother wouldn't like."

Bailey thought, *she was one of them.*

"I've had ice cream for dinner. I put my bare feet on this very table."

"That's one you might have kept to yourself." Bailey took her plate off the table and put it in her lap. Tane laughed and she took notice. Bailey didn't think she ever heard him laugh.

"I did clean the table since I put my feet on it. I even vacuumed."

"Good to know."

They ate their pizza and watched the movie. Tane stretched out on the couch and got her to lay next to him. She rested her head on Tane's chest and the thought of his chest hair right under her head. The movie no longer kept her interest, and she closed her eyes to relive her and Tane in his bed. Bailey was a little mad at herself for stopping Tane. But it was the right thing to do. She rested her hand over his heart and could feel it beating. The last thing she remembered was Tane's beating heart. Her eyes fluttered open and she was still on the couch with Tane. "Oh my God," Bailey jumped up and startled Tane.

"What?"

"We fell asleep. I didn't call my mother. She is going to have a fit. I have to go." Bailey gathered her stuff.

"Tell her we just fell asleep." Tane didn't think it was a big deal.

"Yeah, hey Mom, I slept over at the O'Shea's with Tane with no one home. I can see that going over real well."

"Tell her you watched a movie with me and that I'm taking you to church, after all, I am becoming a priest. Who is the safest person to spend the night with?" Tane put out his arms.

"I'm not sure that's going to go over well, but I'll try it. What time is church?" Bailey was trying to put on her shoes.

"Mass is at ten-thirty, but we have to be there at least fifteen minutes early. Do you want me to pick you up?"

"I'm not sure that's a good idea either. I'll meet you there. If I don't show, then I got in trouble." Bailey gave Tane a quick peck on the cheek and ran out the door.

When Bailey made it home, she knew what would be waiting for her. She yelled out, "Mom, I'm sorry. I fell asleep at a friend's house." Bailey started up the stairs.

"Hold up," her mother came to the bottom of the stairs. "Where were you? Louisa said you went off with a boy."

"Yes, I went to a baseball game with Tane."

"Who?"

"Tane O'Shea, then we went to his house and watched a movie. We fell asleep. I'm sorry I didn't call or text."

"Wait, let me get this straight, you stayed over at the O'Shea's house with Tane? I didn't even know you were friends. Bailey, I think you need to come down here and talk to me."

"Mom," Bailey came down a few stairs. "Tane and I are hanging out. We get thrown together for every O'Shea wedding and we are just getting to know each other."

Her mother squinted her eyes, "Get to know each other, how?"

Bailey rolled her eyes and lied to her mother, "It's not like that. Tane is going off to school soon to start his priesthood. I need to get ready for church. Tane is taking me to Mass."

"You're going to church? With Tane O'Shea?"

"Yes, and I'm really sorry I didn't let you know where I was. But I was as safe as I could be, with Tane." Bailey hoped her mother wouldn't look too deeply into her excuse.

"You're just friends, nothing else?"

"Yes, Mom." Bailey turned so her mother could no longer see her face, "Just friends."

"I want you home after church. I think we need to talk about this new friendship with one of those O'Shea boys."

Bailey rushed up the stairs, "Oh, Mom." She went to her closet and looked for a church-appropriate dress. Bailey went through everything she had and didn't find anything that didn't say sexy young non-virgin. "Crap, I don't have anything to wear." Bailey went through her skirts, and every one of them were too short. She went out of her room and looked down the hall to her parent's room. Bailey quickly moved and slipped inside.

Bailey knew her mother's clothes wouldn't fit her, but she had to find something and quickly. She pulled out a printed wrap dress, something she could tie to fit her. Then Bailey snagged a pair of her mother's old lady shoes. She snuck out of her mother's closet and ran down the hall to her room. Bailey quickly removed the braids in her hair and fluffed it, then added a headband she hadn't had in her hair since fifth grade and slipped into her mother's clothes. When Bailey looked in the mirror she looked like the perfect innocent church-going girl. *It will have to do.*

Tane waited in the outer part of the church. He looked for Bailey every time the door opened. Tane also scanned for any of his family members. He knew they would have a lot of questions about Bailey being in church with him. But that was their problem. He just hoped his brother and Julia wouldn't come today. The later it got the more Tane didn't think Bailey would show. He should have gone home with her and explained how they fell asleep.

The door opened and Tane almost missed her. Bailey had a dress on and didn't look anything like herself. He stepped up to her, "Hey, you made it."

"Barely." Bailey was breathing hard as if she ran the entire way.

Tane leaned down to speak in her ear, "Who's dress do you have on?"

Bailey looked up at him, "I didn't have anything appropriate. I took it from my mother's closet."

Tane smiled, "Let's sit." He led her toward the front of the church.

Bailey stopped walking when she realized where he was going. "Do we have to sit all the way up there? Can't we sit back here?"

Tane thought it might be smart if they didn't sit where the rest of his family sat, "Okay, how about here?" He put out his hand for Bailey to go first.

Bailey shook her head and went into the pew. Tane genuflected and made the sign of the cross on his chest before he sat. Bailey noticed, and asked, "Was I supposed to do that?"

Tane leaned into her side and said, "You don't have to."

"Why do you do it?"

"It shows respect and the love of God." Tane noticed the front pew was empty. He pulled out his phone to check the time. Just then he saw his brother Bryant and Macy come rushing in with the kids. They moved to the front of the church. Grace and Robert were next to come in. The doors to the church were closing when Ray carried one child while Jon had the other and moved to the front pew. It was interesting to see who would come without his parents being there.

Bailey whispered, "You will help me, right? I've only been to the weddings."

Tane took her hand and gave it a squeeze. "I'll make sure you do what you need to do."

The sound of the organ began to play, and everyone stood. Father Joe was led by the altar boys and the Deacon as they moved up the center aisle and the first hymn started. Tane took the book from the little holder, turned to the right page, and began to sing. He put his finger where they were in the song so Bailey could follow along.

Bailey wet her lips and began to sing. She didn't want to be too loud, so she kept her voice low. Tane glanced down at her, and she tried not to feel self-conscious. So, she could sing and read music. Her parents made her take piano lessons when she was a kid.

His Uncle said something, and everyone responded. Bailey mumbled as if she knew what to say. She sat when everyone else did. Tane took out another small red book and opened it for her to see. He whispered, "This is the Mass for today and all the responses you need to know. All you have to do is follow along."

Bailey took the book, and it looked well-worn. She glanced to the front and saw the name, Arlene O'Shea. Bailey said, "This is your mother's and I'm not sure she'd want me to have it."

"My mother would lend her book out to anyone who needed it. Shh, now listen."

Bailey could see all sorts of papers stuck in the pages. She wanted to look through them but had to follow along with the Mass. Bailey stuck her finger in one of the pages she felt something there. She looked at Tane and he was staring forward. Bailey slowly flipped the page. There was a card with a prayer on it, and she turned it over. It had someone's name and date at the bottom.

Tane leaned over and said, "It's a prayer card for someone my mother knew." He felt Bailey move and glanced down just in time to see her snooping through his mother's book.

Bailey quickly put the card back where she found it and felt a little embarrassed that she got caught. She didn't look at anything else and followed along with the readings. Bailey stood when everyone did and knelt when she needed to. There was a lot of up and down to this Catholic service. Tane leaned in again to say, "It's time to receive communion."

"What do I do?"

"Nothing, stay here. Just let everyone move past you."

Bailey watched as each row stood and went to the front. She knew they took bread and wine but didn't get why they received it and what it was all about. She'd have a lot of questions for Tane after Mass.

When it was Tane's turn to stand he moved with his line to the center aisle. He looked at Bailey and smiled. As he got further to the front of the line, Tane knew the second his family saw him they'd wonder why he sat so far back in the church. He had the right to sit anywhere he wanted. But it was the look on his uncle's face when Tane stepped up to receive communion.

"The Body of Christ."

"Amen."

His Uncle broke protocol, and quietly said, "Tane, see me after Mass."

Tane stepped aside and made the sign of the cross as he put the wafer on his tongue and got in line to take the wine. He could feel his family looking at him. Tane moved to his seat as he knew Ray followed him with her eyes. He had no doubt the second Mass was over his sister would be at his seat. Too bad he had to talk to Uncle Joe. Tane didn't want to leave Bailey there to fend for herself. He did something he never did, "Bailey, the second Mass is over we move to the back of the church, okay?"

"What's the matter?"

"Just do it." Tane closed his eyes and told God he was sorry that he wasn't giving him everything he normally did. *I know I've asked you to take the thoughts of Bailey out of my head, and I've tried. Forgive me for my actions. I know they have not been pure. If this is a test, I'm failing miserably. I am only human. I ask you to show me your way. The path I'm supposed to take. In Jesus name, I pray.* Tane sat back on the pew. He could see his sister looking at him.

The second his uncle passed their pew Tane took Bailey's hand and pulled her from their row. He moved down the outside aisle and out the side door.

"Tane what are you doing."

Tane didn't stop moving until they were in the safety of the Parish Hall where the daycare was. "Listen, I don't have long. My Uncle wants to talk to me. I don't want Ray to find you. Go into the bathroom and stay there until I come back for you. Okay?"

"You want me to hide in the bathroom? Tane, do you hear yourself?"

"I don't want you to have to deal with Raylan. Please, Bailey."

"Fine," she agreed to do what he wanted.

Once Bailey was safely tucked away, Tane went to find his uncle. "Uncle Joe, you wanted to see me?"

"Yes, I did. Did you find your sister? It seems she was looking to speak to you also."

"I didn't see Ray."

"How do you know it was Raylan who wanted to talk to you and not Grace? Never mind, I know the answer to that. Can I ask why you sat halfway in the back with your friend?"

Tane decided to tell the truth, "I didn't want anyone asking questions. I guess I didn't avoid that did I? I do have the right to sit where I want to, don't I? It's not written I have to sit in the first row, is it?" When Tane saw his uncle raise a brow, he said, "Bailey didn't feel comfortable sitting in the O'Shea pew."

"Ah, I see. Do I need to have the talk with you about love and lust?"

"I think you do."

Tane was the first of the O'Shea boys to answer yes and it kind of left Uncle Joe speechless.

{7}

Bailey went into one of the stalls and locked the door. She stood there for a long time waiting for Tane to come back. Bailey looked at the red book still in her hand. She knew it wasn't right, but if she had to sit around until Tane came back, then there was time to snoop. Bailey put some paper on the seat of the toilet and sat down. She started at the beginning, turning each page. If something caught her eye, she read it. There were more prayer cards with people's names on them. Bailey thought Tane's mother knew a lot of people who had passed.

There were other things in the book too. Bailey came across a plastic cross with yarn going in and out of the holes. She wondered who made it for Arlene. Bailey turned it over and it had Paul's name on the back. Seeing his name made her smile because thinking of Paul as a child was hard to do. He was a little scary. Paul was more like a brute, and she didn't think anyone would want to meet up with him in a dark alley. Bailey continued turning the pages, she read a few passages and looked through Arlene's mementos. She had something from each of her children in her book. It was nice to see Tane's mother kept all these things. Bailey wondered if her mother ever kept anything she made.

Bailey came to a page that had a folded piece of paper in it. She carefully opened the creased paper. It was a Mother's Day card from Tane. He wrote a poem to his mother in blue crayon. Bailey had to look really hard to see the words. It looked like Tane might have done this when he was five or six years old. The title was Why God Made Mummies.

God made Mummies to love their kids.

Only you love will do.

Deer Mom, you the best!

Happy Mutters Day. Love Tane

Bailey thought how sweet Tane was. He wrote an acrostic poem to his mother. She never remembered being that smart at that age. Bailey took a deep breath and folded the paper back, putting it back inside the book. She stood and didn't think Tane was coming back for her. "I could just go home, but what do I do with Arlene's book? I can't leave it here." *Take it to his house and leave it at the back door. He will surely find it there. After you get home, then text Tane where he can find it. Yep, that'll work.*

Tane was with his uncle a lot longer than he anticipated. He made another appointment to speak to his uncle because he really didn't know what he was doing. Tane went into the Parish Hall. All the lights were out and Tane knew Bailey had most likely left. He knocked on the bathroom door and when no one answered, he pushed the door open, "Bailey. Ah, shit." Tane was supposed to be at the pub already, so he didn't have time to track Bailey down. He pulled out his phone and saw a text from her.

Bailey: I couldn't wait any longer. My mother was expecting me home right after church. I put your mother's book by your back door. I put a rock on it, so nothing blew away.

Tane put his phone away because he had more to say to her than he had time. He hopped in his mother's car and headed for the pub. Tane wasn't looking forward to what Raylan had to say. It didn't matter that he didn't want to hear it, she would stick her nose where it didn't belong. Tane knew most likely the rest of his family would have something to say too. He knew he couldn't keep Bailey a secret forever.

Tane parked his mother's car next to Raylan's. He took a deep breath and banged on the back door. He was glad to see it was Herb and not his sister. Herb said, "Your sister wants to talk to you. It seems everyone is talking about you. Good luck." Herb padded Tane on the shoulder.

Ray spotted Tane, "I see you skipped out right after church."

"I had something to do. What's the big deal?"

"You were with Bailey? When did you two become a couple?"

"Look Ray, I love you and all, but mind your own business."

Herb moved to the other side of the table.

Ray stopped cooking and turned to look at her brother, "Tane what are you doing? Why are you getting caught up with Bailey? You are about to go off to school to become a priest."

"I asked you nicely to mind your own business. I'm an adult and I don't need my big sister sticking her nose in my life. Everyone in this family has done exactly what they wanted. So, bud the fuck out." Tane turned and left the kitchen. He was pissed when he went to the end of the bar. Gabe came over with a big smile on his face.

"So, have you dipped your stick yet? Wet your whistle?"

"What?"

"You know, popped her little cherry. Once you get a taste of some sweet ass you can't go back. I bet she was good."

When Tane realized his brother was talking about Bailey, in a blink of an eye he hurled himself over the bar and jumped on Gabe. Jon who was sitting there said, "Oh, shit and hopped over to try to pull Tane off Gabe. Not that he didn't deserve a punch in the mouth.

"Just because you weren't the first to pop Faith's cherry." Tane got in a few good hits before Mack, Jon, and Patrick broke up the fight. Raylan stood in the doorway of the kitchen watching in disbelief. Mack had Tane in a choke hold as he pulled him out of the bar area and kept going until he had Tane in his office.

Mack pushed Tane down in a chair, "What the hell, Tane?"

"If Gabe talked about Julia the way he was talking about…" Tane wiped the blood from his lip.

"Tane we all saw you kiss Bailey at the baseball game. It was on the TV in the pub." Mack leaned down to look at his brother. "What are you doing?"

Tane yelled, "I want everyone to stop asking me that. I don't know!" His nieces started to cry. They were sleeping in Mack's office. Ray came in and grabbed the two car seats and surprisingly didn't say a word.

Mack sighed, "You might want to figure it out. Bailey is my niece and Julia wasn't happy to see the two of you kissing."

Tane looked up at his brother, "You know what? I don't care what anyone thinks. I did my job and kept my mouth shut when Bryant brought Macy through the kitchen to get her out of here. I never said a word all the times Jon came into the kitchen to mess around with Ray. You, moved Julia upstairs, and I minded my own business. Grace, she moved in with Robert, Gabe does whatever the fuck he wants, Patrick and Ava, do I need to go on. I kept my opinions to myself. But now everyone in this family seems to think they have a right to say what they want. I don't want to hear it." Tane got up and Mack let him walk out. Ray was cooking and didn't look at him. "I'm going home. It doesn't seem you need me. You all have everything under control." Tane slammed the back door to the pub. He sat in his mother's car to cool off before he drove home.

Tane thought *everyone had seen the kiss between him and Bailey. Just great,* he wondered if his parents had seen it too. He was sure the boat had TVs. Tane put his face in his hands. He made a complete and utter mess out of all of this.

Inside the pub, Mack went out to the bar, "Gabe go home, and the next time you come in here, you keep your mouth shut."

"He, jumped, me."

"Get out and be glad I'm not firing you. Patrick, can you run the bar until I get back?"

"Sure."

Mack went back into the kitchen, "Ray, my office." He shut the door. "I don't know what just happened. I have never heard Tane talk so much, much less what came out of his mouth. Tane swore, he said fuck."

"Do you want to know what I think?"

"Yes, that's why I called you in here."

Ray stood by the door, "Well, I was told to mind my own business."

"Yeah, I was too. What's going on with Tane?"

"I think Tane is spreading his wings. He's making a life decision and might be second-guessing himself. He is just nineteen and becoming a priest is…well, a lot. Bailey has had a crush on Tane for as long as she's been around. It was Tane that never gave Bailey the time of day."

Mack sat on the edge of his desk, "What changed?"

"Now, understand I got my information from Gabe."

"Go on."

"I asked Bailey to get some decorations for Julia's baby shower and drop them off at the house. I didn't think at the time that Tane would be home alone. Apparently, Gabe and Faith went over there, unannounced to do some laundry. Gabe asked whose car was in the driveway. Faith said it looked like someone got a haircut in the kitchen. But Bailey was nowhere around. There was a pizza box and an empty beer bottle. Of course, Gabe got all high and mighty asking who was there. Tane said Bailey gave him a haircut. It was no big deal. Gabe went looking for Bailey upstairs and she came out of the downstairs bathroom. Faith ended up dragging Gabe out of the house. The next thing I know, they were kissing on TV."

"Wow, Tane kissing Bailey. You know he was right about each and every one of us. We all did what we wanted."

"Mack, Tane is just a kid. We can't stand by and watch him destroy everything he's worked for."

"Ray, what if he decides not to become a priest? It's his decision to make, right or wrong."

"You know he said fuck when he talked to me. Poor Herb moved around the table afraid of what I might do. I have to admit I was taken back to hear that word come out of his mouth. I didn't even think he knew what it meant."

"Tane has always been so quiet, keeping to himself. Doing whatever was asked of him. But Bailey is still in high school and I'm not sure what Julia's brother's going to say about his daughter seeing Tane."

"What the hell, Mack? Tane's a catch."

"I'd love to find out what Gabe said about Bailey to make Tane go berserk because I might have to punch him myself."

"If you really want to know, ask Jon, he was sitting right there."

Tane pulled into the driveway and when he went to the side door. His mother's missile sat right where Bailey said it would be with the rock sitting on top. Tane took it and the rock inside. He went to the fridge and took out a beer. He didn't care who found out he was drinking it. Tane twisted off the cap and flipped it with his fingers into the sink. On his way to the living room, he put his mother's book on the table. Tane took a big gulp from the bottle. "This has been one hell of a day. Is this you showing me what it's like if I do what I want?" Tane talked to the empty slightly darkened room. "I don't understand why you didn't do this to every one of my siblings. They did what they wanted, and everything worked out fine for them. Is it just me you're fucking with?" Tane took another sip.

It wasn't long before the bottle was empty when Tane went to take another drink. He got up to get one more. The house was too quiet. It was just him and his thoughts. He wanted it all to go away. No thoughts of Bailey or what his family had to say. Tane finished his second beer and went for another. The stress of the day started to wash away as Tane drank his third beer. He felt relief for the first time in days and closed his eyes because they were so heavy. His mind floated, not thinking about anyone or anything.

Ava heard what happened at the pub and the next day she went to the house to check on her brother. Tane and Ava were the closest in age and they were also the last two in the house for a long time. Ava felt she could talk to Tane without him getting angry. She found it hard to think of Tane mad because she had never seen it happen.

When Ava went to unlock the door, the handle turned. Which meant the door wasn't locked. Ava made her way through the mud room and into the kitchen. Everything looked normal, except she noticed her mother's Sunday missile sitting on the table. She found that odd because her mother wasn't home. Ava was afraid to call out to Tane. Her heart pounded in her chest as she crept down the hall until she saw Tane on the couch. He was sitting up but had his eyes closed. Ava didn't see any blood but then saw the beer bottles sitting on her mother's coffee table.

Ava leaned in and said his name. Tane didn't move. "Tane," Ava pushed on his shoulder and was relieved when he was warm to the touch. Tane jumped and his eyes opened.

"Where am I?"

Ava said, "I think you might have gotten drunk last night. I heard you had a tough time of it at the pub yesterday." She sat next to her brother.

"Ah, hell. I have a headache." Tane put his head in his hands.

"I'm sure you do. I'll get you something to take for that. Have you ever drank like this before?"

"Come on, Ava. You know I haven't. I'm the quiet perfect child. I never do anything wrong." Ava handed him two pills and a glass of water. "Thank you."

Ava sat again and didn't say anything. She waited for Tane to say something. "I guess you're here to tell me how I'm screwing up my life like everyone else."

"I didn't say a word. Do you feel like you're screwing things up?"

"To be honest, I have no idea anymore."

"I heard you jumped on Gabe. I bet he was shocked. No one saw that coming. I'm sure Gabe deserved it. But you fighting, never thought it."

"He was running his mouth, and well, I had enough. Everyone has a breaking point."

"Tane, do you want to talk about Bailey. I promise what is said, will stay right here."

Tane said, "Ava, that's just it. I don't know what's going on." He put his head back in his hands. "I'm not sure you want to hear this. I've been thinking about Bailey, like in ways I never thought of anyone."

"What do you mean?"

Tane didn't lift his head, "Sexually. I've had dreams that I won't go into details. I couldn't get her out of my head. I talked to Uncle Joe. I prayed. Nothing worked. Then Bailey showed up here dropping off decorations for the baby shower and I don't know. I invited her to stay, and she cut my hair. We got along great."

"I didn't think you liked Bailey."

"I didn't, not until she stopped looking at me. Then I thought about her wanting someone else and from there I couldn't stop it."

"Does she know... you're a...?"

"I'm a virgin, yes, and I know her status."

"Really, you talked about that?"

"Yes, Ava. Bailey and I talked about a lot of things. I was a little embarrassed at first, but Bailey made me feel normal. A late bloomer but a normal male. How did you navigate through…you know the sex thing? I don't want any details."

"I'm in the same boat as you."

Tane's head popped up. "You are? I thought I was the only one."

"Nope, Daniel and I had that talk early on and he respects me for it."

"Wow, I would have thought that night Mom let you see his friend's band, it would have happened."

"I guess we are the last holdouts."

"Ava, what do I do about Bailey? I don't want to hurt her. I don't want to make a mistake and do something I'll regret. Bailey thinks I will once we…you know."

"Then maybe you shouldn't do it."

"If it was only that easy. I get around her and my body goes into overdrive. I don't know how to control it. It's like God is making me pay big time for having sexual dreams and wanting to…do things."

"Tane, you know God doesn't punish you. I think you're doing that to yourself."

"How did you know you loved Daniel and what you felt for him wasn't just lust?"

"It's hard to explain. I saw a future with him. I look forward to seeing him and I feel like I'm home when I'm with him."

"That doesn't help me. I saw my future clear as a bell and now it's all a fog. Bailey said something to me about getting all the information before making such a big decision. I feel like I owe it to God to give myself to him freely but if I feel the least bit of apprehension, I should listen to it."

"Tane, becoming a priest is a big decision. It's a lifelong thing. It's not like deciding to become a doctor or lawyer. Most kids that go to college don't even go into the field that they went to school for because they find out they don't like it. Some spend hundreds of thousands before they realize it."

"What do I do about school?"

"Listen, you need to go. Put some distance between you and Bailey. The first and second years are all about getting your core classes done. No decision needs to be made now."

"What do I tell her?"

"The truth, you haven't decided. You'll be back for Paul's wedding and Bailey will be there, and again for the holidays."

"I'm not sure how Bailey will take it when I say I'm going off to school."

"Tane, you have four years of college before you can even start the priesthood. There's a lot of time to decide one way or the other."

"I have my classes all around becoming a priest."

"So, you have more religion than most college students." Ava shrugged her shoulders. "Pretty much like growing up in this house. Now, for the beer. I will replace it, so no one has to know, but you have to promise me it won't happen again."

"Thanks, Ava."

{8}

At first, Bailey was glad she hadn't heard from Tane. She didn't want to ignore his text or phone calls. But when one day turned into two and Tane hadn't tried to contact her, she wondered if he was mad at her. In her mind, Bailey went over everything that happened on Sunday. Bailey stood behind the ice cream counter looking out the window. She wasn't looking at anything in particular. It was more of a blur. The only thing she could come up with, Tane was mad she left when he told her to wait for him.

Well, that's tough. I explained why I had to go and if that's not good enough, too bad. He is just going to have to stay mad. Bailey knew her tough attitude was all an act she used to protect herself. And if anyone should be mad, it was her. She was the last one to make contact and he didn't get back to her. Bailey folded her arms over her chest to fortify her resolve. As Bailey's sight cleared, she saw Tane heading her way, and she quickly ducked down.

"I'm not here," Bailey told the other girl she was working with.

The bell over the door rang and her co-worker said, "Hi, welcome to Baskin Robbins. What can I get you?"

Bailey sat on the floor listening, "Hi, I was hoping Bailey was working today?"

"She's not here, but I can help you." Her co-worker leaned on the counter.

Bailey looked up at her co-worker because it sounded like she was flirting with Tane.

"Thanks, I'll try her at home." Tane turned and left the store. Bailey peaked over the counter to watch him leave.

"He's cute. Why didn't you want to talk to him?"

"It's complicated. Were you flirting with him?" Bailey imitated her co-worker's voice, "She's not here, but I can help you."

"And he didn't even take a second look before leaving. I think you're safe."

"But now he's going to my house and what if they tell him I'm working? He's going to know I ditched him." Bailey would stick to her plan and not contact Tane. She knew he would eventually catch up to her. But she needed some time to figure out what she wanted.

When Bailey got off from work, she looked at her phone and there were no messages from Tane. So, he hadn't tried to contact her. She went about her way and tried not to think about him. Bailey decided she needed a little pick-me-up. On her way home she stopped at the beauty supply. After all, they say blondes have more fun. Bailey knew going from chestnut brown to blonde would take a long process and a lot of bleaching, but she never colored her hair before so she knew it could be done.

Tane had a feeling Bailey was avoiding him. After he went to her house and was told she wasn't home. He didn't know if that was true or not, but he didn't see her car anywhere when he drove around the block to look. *So, if she's not at work and not at home, where could she be?* Tane wanted to talk to her in person and not have this conversation over the phone. He didn't know how she would take him telling her he planned to go off to college and would go forward as before. Tane had four years to decide if the priesthood was right for him. Once he left, Tane was sure his mind would clear, but he didn't know what that meant for him and Bailey. Would she still want to be friends or would things go back to the way they were? Tane wanted them to be at least friends. In the short time they've been hanging out together, Bailey had become very important to him. She was the first girl he ever had a real conversation with, and now she was avoiding him.

"Great job, O'Shea." Tane took out his phone.

Tane: I need to talk to you.

He hit send and waited. "Maybe I should send her flowers? No, I can't do that. Where would I send them? I could sit on her front steps until she comes home. Bailey has to come home sometime."

Tane found a parking spot where he could see her house and planned to wait her out.

Bailey got all her supplies to make her dramatic change. She parked her car on the street behind her house and walked through the alley. Bailey saw Tane's text but decided not to respond. Did she really need to hear Tane wanted to break things off? "It's a good thing I didn't have sex with him. That would be the first good move you made since you rang the O'Shea's doorbell." Bailey went in the back door and headed for her room. The next time she left the house her hair would be blonde. "Well, as blonde as I can get it without completely frying my hair, that is."

Bailey went into her bathroom and began mixing the bleach packets with the thirty-volume developer. She made sure to have one of her mother's white towels so as not to strip the color out of a colored one. Bailey stood in front of the mirror in her bra and underwear putting the mixture on her head. She scooped the white paste from the bowl and made sure to spread it evenly. Once she was happy with the coverage, Bailey put the bag over her hair. She'd check it every ten minutes because she wanted to go at least three levels lighter.

Bailey went into her room and put on some music. She began to sing and dance around. The thought of her singing in church and how Tane looked at her came to mind. She shrugged the thought away. Her phone went off for her first hair check. Bailey found her hair was lifting faster than she thought it would. That was good. It meant less damage to her hair. She fastened the bag back into place with a clip.

Tane sat in his mother's car for hours with no sign of Bailey. He was getting hungry and had to find a bathroom. When he decided to move, he knew he'd lose his spot. But he didn't have a choice. Tane drove to the closest fast-food restaurant and ordered a burger and fries. After he relieved his bladder, Tane returned to Bailey's house. He had to drive around the corner to find a parking place, and that's when he saw her car. So, she was home. Tane parked and walked to her front steps, pulling out his phone.

Tane: I know you're home. I need to talk to you, and I'll be waiting for you out front. If you don't come out, then I'll ring the bell.

Tane hated giving her an ultimatum, but she didn't leave him much choice. He walked back and forth past her steps looking at his phone for her response.

Bailey heard her phone and picked it up, "Oh, shit." She grabbed a hat, tucked all her hair under it, and rushed down the stairs. Bailey didn't want Tane to ring the bell and alert her parents that he was there. She opened the door and saw Tane standing on the sidewalk. Bailey moved down the stairs and stood in front of him. "Let's walk." She moved in next to him.

He asked, "Did you get my text?"

"I did, but I was busy."

"Where were you? I stopped by work, and I came here."

"Last I checked, I don't have to report to you about my whereabouts."

"Okay, I get it you're avoiding me," Tane stopped walking, "Bailey, we need to talk."

"Let me guess, you're breaking whatever this is off, and you still want to be friends. Look, this isn't my first time doing this. I'll save you the…"

Tane kissed Bailey to get her to stop talking. Her hat fell off her head. "What did you do to your hair?" Tane took a piece of her blonde hair in his fingers.

Bailey stepped back breaking their connection. "I changed it. I'm allowed to do that. It's my hair."

Tane grabbed Bailey's shoulder and pulled her into the dark alleyway. "Why are you acting this way? Why did you feel the need to get rid of your beautiful brunette hair? Bailey, talk to me."

"Tane, why don't you tell me what was so important." Tane didn't say anything. "That's what I thought."

"Bailey, come back to my house so we can talk."

Bailey pushed Tane, "Not a chance. I've been down that road. Anything you have to say to me, you can do it right here."

"Look, I know I made a mess of all this. I don't know the protocol." Bailey laughed and said the word "protocol" under her breath. "I told you I didn't know what I was doing."

"But you've come to your senses. I'm not good enough. That's fine, you don't want to hurt my feelings, blah, blah, blah. I'm so glad I had enough sense to not have sex with you. I knew you'd do this." Bailey shook her head as she felt the tears stinging in her eyes. "I have to go. Don't worry about me, I'm fine. Go do your priest thing." Bailey started sidestepping Tane so she could get away from him.

"It's not like that, Bailey. Please don't go."

Bailey said over her shoulder, "Tane you don't want to add lying to your sins since you met…whatever." She rushed to get inside before Tane tried to stop her. Bailey went straight to her room. She turned off her phone and climbed into her bed. That's where she let the tears fall.

Tane stood there knowing he just fucked up royally. *I guess the problem of telling her is solved. Oh goodie.* Tane went to his car and once again drove home to an empty house. Being alone was becoming a real drag.

Over the next few days, Tane tried to contact Bailey with no response. Her phone went straight to voicemail. He could go to her job, but what would he say to her? Tane actually felt guilty for the way he treated Bailey. He never hurt someone's feelings before, and he didn't like the person he was becoming. Tane went back to being a hermit. He went to work and did what was expected of him. Tane didn't speak to anyone until they said something to him.

The day his parents came home everyone gathered at the house. Ray made a big dinner to celebrate their homecoming. Tane came down from his room to eat and then slipped away once it was over. He avoided any contact with his sister-in-law, Julia. He didn't need to see the disapproval in her eyes. It wasn't unusual behavior for him.

Arlene detected something wrong and asked her daughter, "Raylan, what's going on with Tane?"

Ray didn't want to look at her mother, she acted as if she was busy rinsing the dishes before putting them in the dishwasher. "What do you mean?"

"Raylan, what happened while we were gone?"

Raylan turned off the water, "Tane started hanging out with Bailey. There were a few…things. But I don't think they're talking anymore."

"Things?"

"Mom, I don't want to tell you because it isn't my place. I think you should talk to Tane." Raylan quickly moved out of the kitchen before her mother pressed her for more.

Arlene went up to Tane's room and knocked on the door. "May I come in?" She pushed his door open. Tane sat up on his bed.

"What's up?"

"I hear you hung out with Bailey while we were gone. Do you want to talk about it?"

"Not really. I don't know what you were told. But call it a misjudgment on my part and I'd like to move past it."

"I see. So, you don't want to be the one to tell me what happened? You do know, I will find out."

"It really sucks that everyone in this family are adults and still feel the need to tattle. I could tell you stories about every member of this family that would make…." Tane looked at his mother, "Never mind."

"Bailey is your brother's niece, and we see her family."

"I realize that, but you won't need to worry. I didn't have sex with her or anything."

Arlene's eyes got big, "Sex? Tane, where did that come from?"

"Nothing, pretend I didn't say that. I'm still as pure as the day I was born. That's what everyone seems to be worried about."

Arlene closed the door and sat on the bed next to her son. "I think we need to talk."

Tane didn't want to have this conversation with his mother. He wanted to tune her out. "I spent some time with Bailey. We went to a baseball game, and we kissed because they put the kiss cam on us. End of story." Tane figured that wasn't a lie. Of course, he was leaving a whole lot out.

"Tane look at me."

"I don't want to. Mom, this isn't a conversation a male child wants to have with his mother."

"I see, so it evoked feelings in you that you weren't prepared to feel."

"Something like that."

"Tane, that's normal."

"Apparently, not for me."

"Why not you? Last I checked you are human and have feelings like everyone else. You might keep your emotions close, but Tane you aren't immune from feeling."

"I'm not allowed to feel something for a girl because I'm becoming a priest. That's what everyone expects of me." Tears began to fill Tane's eyes, "I'll let everyone down if I don't."

Arlene's heart broke for her son, she put her arms around him and pulled him in tight. "You could never let your father and I down. If you choose to become a priest, wonderful, and if you don't that's okay too. Tane, we want your happiness most and foremost. Putting your happiness first is not being selfish. I would not want you to become a priest if it wasn't truly what you wanted."

Tane pulled back, "I'm going forward with my schooling. I think once I get away from here, Bailey will be just a memory."

Arlene knew Tane had a hard road ahead of him. She would support him in any decision he made, but she had a feeling it wouldn't be what her son thought it would be.

The day came for Tane to leave for school. No one brought up Bailey's name and he was glad. He knew she didn't want to have anything to do with him and it was what was best for him right now. His parents drove him to the out-of-state campus and helped him get settled in. Tane hugged his mother and then his father and said goodbye. At least until he came home for his brother's wedding. Tane wasn't looking forward to it because she would be there. He didn't know how he should act and knew everyone would be watching them.

Tane hoped time did heal all wounds.

Bailey bounced back as she always did once school started. It was her senior year after all and time to have fun. She kept her blonde hair mostly because of his reaction to it. It was her way of saying who cares. Bailey worked hard to balance her schoolwork and her classes to finish getting her cosmetology license. Once she got enough class time, she started working in the school salon cutting real people's hair. Bailey had to give up her job at the ice cream place. There just wasn't enough time in the day. Plus, she wanted to do things with her friends.

The day of her aunt's baby shower came, and Bailey told her mother she wasn't feeling well. "Bailey, you're going to miss Julia's shower. All those cute baby outfits."

"I don't think it's a good idea to go if I'm not feeling well. I could give it to Aunt Julia. She has enough going on with her back hurting. I don't want to make her sick." Her mother motioned as if she understood. Bailey just didn't want to see the O'Shea's. Not one of them called her to see how she was doing, and they weren't her family just because her aunt married into the family. If she could, Bailey would back out of being in Tane's brother's wedding. It wasn't like Paul or Lauren would miss her. Once her mother was out the door, Bailey said, "Let Tane get his own fill-in girl." She went up to her room to get some homework done.

Arlene held the shower at her house. Everything was set up for a wonderful afternoon. As the guests started to arrive, Arlene greeted everyone. Bailey's mother came in and Arlene noticed Bailey wasn't with her.

"Hello Robin, I'm glad you could make it. Where's Bailey?"

"Oh, she wasn't feeling well and of course, we don't want to give anything to Julia."

"I see." Arlene knew exactly what Bailey's problem was, she didn't want to face the O'Shea's. *I'll have to fix that.* "How's Bailey enjoying her last year of high school?"

"She's keeping busy. Bailey is now working in the school salon cutting hair. I lined up a job for her when she graduates in my favorite salon. She should do well there."

"That's wonderful."

"How's Tane doing? I know he and Bailey spent some time together over the summer. He even took her to church." Bailey's mother leaned in to speak quietly to Arlene. "At first, I thought something was going on between the two, but I was wrong."

Arlene thought, *I don't think you were.* "Tane is doing well at school. He's looking forward to coming home for Paul's wedding. What school is Bailey in? I'd love to go and support her by having her cut my hair."

"Oh, that would be wonderful. I know Bailey would love that."

Robin gave Arlene all the information she needed to stop by and have a little talk with Bailey. Not that she planned to interfere, just let Bailey know she was always welcomed in the O'Shea household.

It was nice to know Tane took Bailey to church. That made Arlene feel, a little better about what she found out about Tane and Bailey's time spent together.

{9}

Bailey broke her silence once Arlene O'Shea left after getting a haircut.

Bailey: Your mother showed up tonight to get a haircut. What did you tell her?

Tane's phone never went off, so he was shocked to see Bailey's name come up.

Tane: I didn't tell her anything. What did she want?

Bailey: Your mother wanted me to know I'm always welcome at your house. What the hell?

Tane: Why would my mother randomly show up to get a haircut. How would my mother know where you went to school?

Bailey: I didn't go to Julia's baby shower and apparently your mother talked to my mother about how we spent some time together over the summer.

Tane: I'm sorry if my mother made you feel uncomfortable. I'm sure that wasn't her intention. I'm sure she wanted you to know you are still welcome at my house.

Bailey: It would be weird to be there after…

Tane: Once again, I'm sorry. How are you?

Bailey: Fine, and you?

Tane: So, we're down to small talk now?

Bailey: I guess we are. I didn't mean to bother you. I just got a little freaked.

Tane: Bother me anytime. I miss talking to you.

Bailey: I gotta go. Have a good night.

Tane looked at Bailey's last response. It was right there in a nutshell. I gotta go. What could he say to that? At least it broke the ice, and he knew she would at least speak to him at the wedding. It would be not having her in his arms again that would be the hard part. He knew Bailey would keep him at arm's length. Tane closed his eyes and let the thoughts of her play like a movie through his mind.

Tane had checked her social media page more times than he wanted to admit when he missed her. He would lie in bed looking at her pictures. Tane knew Bailey had kept her blonde hair. He saw her having fun with her friends. There wasn't anything new on his page because he didn't have anything exciting to post. Bailey was the biggest thing to happen to him and he screwed it up.

Tane shook the thought of what might have been and went back to writing his paper that was due in a few days.

The weeks passed and Tane packed a bag to head home for his brother's wedding. He would get in just in time for the rehearsal. Tane hoped his flight wouldn't be delayed. Not that if he missed the rehearsal in the church, he wouldn't know what to do. But if he was being truthful, he was looking forward to seeing Bailey. Tane got to the airport and on his flight without any problems. He kinda of wished he decided to go to school closer to home.

When Tane's plane landed he walked off with just his overnight bag. His stay would be a short one. Besides, he had plenty of clothes at home. Tane grabbed a cab and told the driver the address to the church. He paid the cabbie and got out. Tane totally understood why no one could pick him up at the airport because everyone was tied up with the wedding. Tane had to take the last fight out because he had a late class.

Tane took a deep breath as he pulled the church door open. He saw his Uncle Joe, first. "Tane! You made it. Just in time." His uncle gave him a tight hug.

"You know, I wouldn't miss an O'Shea wedding." Tane looked beyond his uncle. Bailey stood at the front of the church. He wanted to go straight to her but resisted the urge. He lost that right to go up and hug her.

"Go say hello to everyone." His uncle smiled as if he knew what Tane was thinking. It was weird how his mother and uncle did that. He greeted everyone with hugs and handshakes. Tane made his way closer to her, until she turned away and started talking to Faith. He knew this was hard on her too. He didn't handle things right, but he hoped Bailey would give him another chance. *To talk...just talk...yeah right.*

"Okay, everyone is here. I'd like all of you in the back of the church," Father Joe announced. "I know most of you know what to do, but Lauren's brothers aren't as well rehearsed as the rest of you. So, bear with me. Okay, we will start with the ushers," Uncle Joe waved his hands to have them move forward. "You will seat the guests. When everyone is seated, Mack will escort his mother to her spot in the front row." Father Joe put out his hand for Mack to walk his mother to her seat. "Once all the guests are seated the ushers will join Paul at the front of the church. Please walk on the outside so as not to distract from where the bride will be or mess up the runner." He waved his hands. Everyone moved as he asked.

Tane stood in front of the church watching Bailey. She was always first to come down the aisle. He noticed she had on a long dress as she did that day, he asked her to go to church with him. Tane was hoping to catch her eye. But Bailey walked down without looking at him. He needed to bide his time because he knew he'd get to touch her when they had to walk down the aisle. Tane thought about the day she'd walk down the aisle on her wedding day. Would he be the groom or the priest? *You won't be there.* Tane rubbed his chest at the thought.

Uncle Joe went on and on about different parts of the ceremony and how Mass would go. Tane turned so he could see her, and Bailey was looking at her hands. He yelled, "Stop talking and let me talk to my girl." Tane shook and everyone was in the same place and Uncle Joe was still talking. *I guess I just said that in my head. Besides, she's not your girl.* The reality was sobering. In about five minutes he'd get to touch her and then the rehearsal would be over. They still had dinner, but he knew she'd stay clear of him. He had to get her alone.

"Okay, now I say you may kiss…"

Paul already had Lauren bent over in a dip and kissing her. When they came up for air, Lauren said, "I do." And everyone laughed.

"Okay everyone walk out with your partner, yada, yada, yada. You know the drill." Uncle Joe waved his hands as if he dismissed everyone.

To Tane's dismay, no one was doing it. Everyone just walked off the altar. Arlene said, "Dinner is at my house."

Tane moved closer to Bailey, "Hey, do you have a minute?"

Bailey looked around and said, "Sure."

Tane tried to move them aside, but Bailey didn't go. "I know this is hard for you and I'm not trying to make it any harder. But I'd really like it if we could at least talk to each other."

"You mean, like friends. Been there done that. Look, Tane you didn't want me in your life so why are you so worried about staying friends. Do you feel guilty for the way you treated me, perhaps? Don't, because I am over you."

When Bailey started to walk away, Tane grabbed her arm. "I let you get away once."

Bailey looked around and everyone was gone. "So, say whatever it is you need to make yourself feel better."

Tane pulled her into him, "I love you," and he kissed her. He let her go and walked out leaving her standing there in shock. Once Tane made it outside, he realized he had no ride home.

Bailey stood at the top of the church steps, "Do you need a ride?"

Tane turned and said, "I think I do…and I left my bag in the church." Bailey held up his bag, and Tane said, "Right, so much for dramatic exits."

Bailey came down the stairs and said, "I'm still mad at you. So, don't think that kiss makes up for everything."

"I did tell you I loved you. Does that mean anything to you?" They walked to Bailey's car.

"It's a start. But if it doesn't change anything, then you should have kept it to yourself." Bailey unlocked the doors.

Tane sat in the passenger seat. He had her undivided attention. "Bailey, I missed you, a lot. I miss having you there to talk to, and my best friend. That night you dropped off the decorations, you said you like to talk, and I said, I don't need to fill the air with unnecessary words. These months away from you made me realize

94

how much I hate being alone. How much I liked talking…to you. I laughed and smiled more when I was with you than I ever have. Bailey, I want you in my life." Tane leaned in to do what he'd wanted to do since the day he left. He kissed her with everything he had. Bailey kissed him back. He reached for her seat to recline it and it wasn't long before Tane was on top of her.

Bailey broke the kiss, "Tane, you don't want to do this here…"

Tane looked around, "I know where we can go." He stopped, "Are you with me, Bailey?"

She blinked a few times and said, "Yes." Tane took her hand and led her to the Parish Hall. He put in the code and opened the door. "How did you know how to get in."

"My uncle is the priest here, and my mother cleans the church all the time." Tane left the lights off as he moved them into the kitchen pantry. It was the only place Tane knew there were no cameras. "Bailey, are you sure you want to do this? I don't…" she kissed him. All common sense went right out the window.

Tane wanted to touch every part of her body. "Bailey, I want you. I need to…" Bailey pulled his shirt out of his pants. "How do I get you out of this dress?" She reached for the hem and pulled it over her head. Bailey stood there in her bra and panties. "Oh, God forgive me. I can't help myself." Tane kissed down her neck and over her breast. He slipped the cup aside and his mouth covered her nipple. He groaned. Bailey's head fell back as she leaned against the shelves full of food. Bailey moved her hands up inside his shirt and Tane felt like his skin was on fire.

Tane took ahold of Bailey's ass, and he lifted her, sitting her on the shelf. Canned food hit the ground but that didn't stop them. He tried to get his pants open, but he didn't want to stop touching her. "I don't have…any." Tane shifted her thong to one side. His world was about to shatter but he didn't care. He had to be inside her. Tane lined up his body to hers and slid home. "Mother fucker. God, Bailey." She started moving and Tane thought he died and gone to heaven. They worked together and Tane heard her say, "Pull out before you come." Her words didn't register in his brain until his body couldn't take it anymore. Bailey tried to get him to move back, but Tane was out of it.

"Tane, you have to pull out!"

Tane looked at her and saw the distress on her face and he pulled out, but it was a little too late. "I'm sorry, I didn't..."

Bailey fixed her underwear. "I'm sure it will be alright. Let me go to the bathroom." She grabbed her dress off the floor and put it over her head. Bailey left the small space.

Tane stood there with his pants still open and wondered what had come over him. He didn't know if he should have said something to Bailey or was letting her go the right thing to do. Tane tucked his shirt in and zipped up his pants. He picked up all the cans off the floor and put them back on the shelf. Tane decided he needed to go check on Bailey.

Tane opened the door and whispered her name, "Bailey, are you okay?" He went inside the ladies room and found the stall door that was locked. "Bailey, talk to me. I don't know what I'm supposed to say or do. Please."

"I'm fine. It's just that we didn't use any protection and well, you didn't really pull out. The good news is I think you can only get pregnant like four days out of a month. The odds are in our favor."

Tane put his forehead on the door. "What do we do now?"

"We pretend this never happened because we still have dinner to get through."

"I'm not sure I can do that. I...I mean we just..."

She finished his sentence, "Had sex."

Tane frowned, "I wouldn't call it just sex."

"Tane, that's what you do in a car or a closet. People that make love are in a committed relationship and they usually do it in a bed. In their house. Not ripping each other's clothes off in a storage room."

"I'm sorry, I took you in the closet because it was the only place that doesn't have cameras."

"You've got to be kidding me. We are on camera coming in here?" Bailey closed her eyes. How did she get herself into these predicaments? "Tane, I will take you home. Tell your mother I'm sorry I couldn't come for dinner."

"No Bailey. If you don't go, then neither will I. I'm not leaving you. We're in this together."

Bailey knew if she turned up pregnant, she wouldn't tell him. "Your mother will miss you. I'm just a stand-in. I'm sure no one will miss me."

"I'm not leaving you. I'll tell my mother we got caught up talking."

"So, you're going to lie? To your mother?"

"It's not a lie. We are talking."

"Tane."

"Please come out so I don't have to keep talking to you through the door." Bailey unlocked it and came out. Tane pulled her into his arms. "We should get out of here. I don't want to rush you...but."

"We're on camera."

"Well, not in here." Tane tilted Bailey's face up to his, "I missed you."

"You said that already," Bailey looked into Tane's eyes.

"I know, but I want you to know how much. I plan to finish out this semester and then transfer to a local college so we can be together."

"Tane, you really want to do that? What are your parents going to say?"

"Bailey, I know my parents will be shocked and concerned. But they won't stop me from switching schools."

"And becoming a priest?"

"You helped me realize I don't like being a solitary person. I don't want to hide in my room anymore. I want someone to share my life with me. I want you by my side."

Bailey smiled, "I can't believe you're saying all this. I thought once you left...well, you didn't look back."

"You changed me, Bailey Mealey."

Father Joe felt his phone go off. Even though he was at a family function, he had to check it. People called on him at all times of the day and night. When a call came in to give someone last rights, Father Joe dropped everything else. He saw there was a notification that the door to the Parish Hall had been opened. Joe walked away from the group to look at the video. No alarms were going off so the code on the door had to be entered.

In the dark, he saw two figures move through the main dining hall and into the kitchen and then they disappeared. Joe had a good idea who had entered the Parish Hall. He kept watching after one left the kitchen and went into the bathroom. Joe took a deep breath when he zoomed in on the other figure and knew it was Tane.

"Is everything alright, Joe?" Cadman had seen his brother looking at his phone.

Joe slipped his phone into his pocket, "Everything is…it's probably nothing." He noticed that Tane and Bailey never made it back from the rehearsal. "Cadman, you might want to have a talk with your son. I won't divulge anything that's been said, but I've always reserved the right to come to you if I thought it necessary."

Cadman looked at his brother, "Is there a particular son I should be speaking to?"

"Yes, the one that's not here," Joe walked away.

When Bailey dropped Tane off, the house was dark. Tane hoped he wouldn't have to explain why he didn't make it to dinner. He hoped no one would notice he wasn't there. As Tane moved through the kitchen and down the hall he heard his father's voice. "You never made it back here for your brother's rehearsal dinner." A light came on and Tane saw his father sitting on the couch.

"Yeah, I'm sorry about that. Bailey and I had a few things to straighten out. I made a mess of things before I left."

"And you resolved everything?"

"Yes, Sir. I felt I owed her that much."

"I see, and where do you stand with this young lady who's still in high school."

Tane closed his eyes, "I'm not sure you remember your first kiss, but things change."

"Oh, I doubt that. I remember my first real kiss like it was yesterday. Your mother kissed me in the library and knocked my socks off. But son, you can't let one kiss change your entire life. I know the power of the female scent. It gets into your head and scrambles your brain. You're a man now and you have to keep your emotions in check."

"That kiss was more powerful than I ever thought it could be. But what do I know because I only kissed one girl."

"Your mother had a similar dilemma because she too only kissed me. Her thought was if she kissed someone else, she'd know if what she felt for me was real. I wasn't happy about the idea or the person she chose. As it turned out she thought better of it and trusted her gut. I found out later the other boy would have loved to kiss your mother, but I found her first."

Tane frowned, "Oh, ew. Tell me it wasn't Uncle Joe who wanted to kiss Mom?"

Cadman laughed, "Where did you come up with your uncle?"

"He told me there was this girl he wanted to kiss but his friend saw her first and he went off to college and that was the end of that. I asked if he still saw his "Friends," and he said, all the time. Oh, I think I might be sick." Tane rubbed his stomach.

Cadman became serious, "Son, I want you to realize adult actions come with adult consequences."

"I understand," Tane went up to his room. He took a few minutes to let it sink in, he had sex with Bailey. Tane heard his father go to bed and decided to take a shower. He could hear his parents talking as he stood in the hall.

"Tane knows it was my brother who wanted to kiss you."

"Oh my, goodness, no. Besides your brother was so relieved when I told him I wasn't kissing him."

His father laughed, and Tane heard the ruffling of the bed sheets. "Oh, he wanted you, but you were mine. I knew the moment I saw you. But that kiss in the library sealed the deal."

Tane heard his mother laugh and he went into the bathroom. *That's what I want for myself.*

{10}

The morning of the wedding all the guys got ready at the O'Shea house and all the girls were at Lauren's apartment. Tane was ready for the wedding to be over and have Bailey in his arms. He stood back as he always did, and no one looked at him any differently than before he had sex with Bailey. *That's because they don't know, and they won't.*

After he and Bailey talked for hours last night, they decided to play it cool. They would walk together when expected, and dance when they were supposed to. They figured after everyone had a drink or two, no one would notice them. Tane was good at fading into the background, Bailey on the other hand always stood out. At least she did to him.

"What are you smiling at?"

Tane looked at his brother, "Was I smiling? I didn't realize." He closed his mouth. "Is that better?"

"You know there's something different about you since you went off to school. Did you grow an inch or two?" Patrick stood close to his brother. "No, I don't think that's it."

"Patrick, why do you care? Why are you even looking at me? Stop it, or I'll wait up in my room, until it's time to go."

"That's it…you're here with the rest of us and not in your room."

"I'm expected to be here, otherwise I'd be in my room. Now, go away." Tane watched Patrick walk away. He saw Gabe standing on the other side of the room. They hadn't spoken since the fight at the pub. Gabe didn't apologize often to anyone. Tane didn't see what Faith saw in his brother. The next time Tane saw Faith, he apologized to her for what he said about her during the fight even though she wasn't there. He felt it was the right thing to do. Faith said she understood, and she was sorry that Gabe said those things about Bailey. Tane told her it wasn't up to her to apologize for his brother.

Tane pulled on the cuffs of his sleeves to relieve the tension he felt under his suit jacket. He watched his brother Bryant marry Macy, and Mack marry Julia. His sister, Ray married Jon, and Grace to Robert. Now, Paul will make Lauren an official family member. There were three more weddings being planned. He didn't know who would be next? Tane thought it would be one of his twin brothers. He didn't keep up with those kinds of things and just showed up where he was told to be. It wouldn't hurt his feelings none if Gabe chose not to ask him to be a part of his wedding.

Mack stepped up to Tane. He looked in the direction Tane was staring. "How are you doing?"

Tane blinked and looked at his brother, "Fine, and you?"

Mack smiled, "I'm sure being back has brought up some uncomfortable feelings."

"Are you talking about Gabe or Bailey?"

"Both, I know Gabe is a dick sometimes."

"He's a jackass all the time. But we're all adults here, right?"

"It doesn't make it right. Did he ever say…"

"No, not a word, and you know what, I like it that way." Someone started yelling it was time to get to the church. Tane said, "Here we go. One more O'Shea down, three more to go."

Mack put his hand on Tane's shoulder, "I think you mean four more," His brother slipped his arm around him, and they walked toward the front door together. It wasn't lost on Tane, his brother's meaning. Everyone piled into the limos, Tane sat next to his oldest brother and for the first time, he was starting to feel as if he was a part of this family. When they arrived at the church there were so many groomsmen that they all wouldn't fit in the small space the church set aside for them.

Tane stood outside between the church and the Parish Hall. It wasn't long before Robert and Daniel joined him. "It's a little too loud in there," Robert said.

"And too many people," Daniel added.

"You best get used to that," Tane said.

Jon and Patrick were next to come outside. "I love your brother, but Paul is off the chain in there," Jon said when they joined the group.

Tane was hoping to be alone before the wedding started. He saw Gabe come out the door and decided to go back inside. As he passed his brother Gabe said, "Tane, you got a minute." Tane stopped walking and turned to face his brother but didn't say a word.

"I'm sorry for the things I said about…you know."

"Bailey?"

"Yeah, that was me just being an asshole. I like Bailey."

"Do you even know her?" Tane took a deep breath, "I accept your apology. Gabe, you don't have to always be a jerk about things."

"I know, I'm working on it."

"Did Faith make you apologize?"

"Let's just say, she made me see my error."

"She's good for you, although I don't know what she sees in you."

"I wonder about that myself sometimes." Gabe reached out his hand for Tane to shake. He took it. "I do want you to be happy, Tane. We all deserve that."

"Oh, look they kissed and made up," Patrick yelled.

"Shut up, Patrick. Having one jerk in the family is enough." Tane walked back inside.

"Has anyone noticed how much Tane is talking? Or am I the only one?" Everyone said, "Shut up, Patrick."

Tane made his way to the other side of the church, where he knew the girls were. There were a few females standing outside smoking. They were Lauren's brother's girlfriends. Tane didn't even know their names. He knocked on the door to the bride's suite, Ray came to the door, "Can I help you?"

Tane said, "Can I speak…," and Ray yelled over her shoulder for Bailey. Ray winked at him and shut the door. Tane smiled because his sister could be a real drag if she wanted to be, but when she was on your side it was the best.

Bailey opened the door and stepped out into the hallway. She looked so pretty in her baby blue strapless dress. "Wow, you look great!"

"Thanks, Tane. You don't look so bad yourself."

"I know we agreed to play it cool and all. But I wanted to see you before…everything." Bailey smiled up at him, and he looked around, taking her hand in his. "Can I kiss you?"

Bailey looked down the hall, "I don't think anyone will know." She stepped up to him and went up on her tippy toes to kiss him.

"I look forward to our dance."

"What a big change from the last wedding."

"I was watching you dance on the dance floor all by yourself. I saw your every move."

"Yes, but then you didn't like it."

"I think I did because if I didn't, I wouldn't have looked your way. I would have found a quiet place to wait for the wedding to be over."

"My little introvert." Bailey went in for one more kiss. "I better get back inside before anyone misses me." They both laughed. It was like their private joke. Tane went back to the groom's side of the church, and they were getting ready to start walking guests down the aisle. This wasn't his favorite thing to do, but he did it anyway. Because the wedding was taking place during Saturday Mass, they walked every old lady to their seat. The only good thing about Lauren having three brothers was there were more guys to choose from. Tane stood back and only took his turn when someone picked him to walk them to their seat.

When it was time, all the groomsmen stood in the front of the church. The music began to play, and his uncle and a small procession came up the aisle. Mass began as usual and then the wedding would start after his uncle said a few words.

"We are blessed with these two who will become as one in the eyes of God. In his house, let this union be timeless." The music began and the back doors of the church opened up. Bailey stood there and slowly made her way down the aisle. Tane's eyes stayed glued to her. She smiled as she made her way up to the altar. Next came the three women Tane didn't know, and then Shana, Faith,

Ava, Grace, and Ray. If this family got any bigger, a wedding could take hours.

The music changed and Lauren and her father appeared. Tane glanced at his brother, Paul, and watched as he pulled a hanky from his pocket to wipe his eyes. It moved Tane to see his brother show his emotions this way. Paul always came off as a strong, tough male. As Lauren got closer, Tane thought she looked beautiful. He looked Bailey's way and she too seemed to be moved by the wedding because she wiped her eyes.

"Who gives this woman to be wed?"

Lauren's father said, "I do." He lifted Lauren's veil and kissed her forehead. He then put his daughter's hand in Paul's. His brother kissed the back of her hand before they moved further up on the altar. It was a small gesture but meant so much. Tane thought he never paid that much attention to those small details before.

Uncle Joe went through his normal routine, but this time Tane listened to his uncle's words about marriage whereas other times he just tuned him out. It was almost as if it never pertained to him because he never planned to get married. It was like an entire new world had just opened up for him. The pledge his brother made to Lauren and hers to him was so meaningful.

Before Tane knew it, his uncle was giving out communion. He stepped up to him and said, "The Body of Christ."

"Amen." Tane put out his hands for his uncle to put the wafer in them and noticed how his uncle didn't look at him as he always did when he received communion. Tane realized he needed to confess his sins before receiving, but there was no time. *I should have crossed my arms over my chest and not received.* It felt so natural to receive, he didn't give it any thought because he never really did anything bad. He had to make this right. There wasn't any time today and very little tomorrow before he had to catch his flight out. Tane wondered how his uncle knew.

The time came when Bailey joined Tane to walk out of the church. He didn't do anything differently than he ever did before. Bailey put her arm through his and they walked out of the church. Every other couple did the same until his brother and his wife started the greeting line just beyond the church doors.

Bailey looked up at him and asked, "What's wrong?"

"What makes you think something's wrong?"

"One, you answered my question with a question. Two, you're all tense."

"I'll tell you later when no one is watching us."

"It's that bad?"

Tane leaned down to speak into Bailey's ear, "It's bad for me. I received communion when I shouldn't have, because of..."

"Oh, but no one knows about...that."

"God knows, and I think my uncle. I don't know how he knows but he does."

"Oh," people started coming through the line, Tane and Bailey smiled as they walked by. "What are you going to do?"

"I don't know...yet."

"Are you going to talk to him? I mean like confess? Then everyone will know." Bailey smiled as people walked by them. They were always at the end of the line and people pretty much just walked by them.

"If I confess to my uncle, he can't tell anyone. If I go to someone else, well, how he knows or what he knows is fair game."

"Oh, God."

"Pretty much."

Once the line ended everyone went back into the church for pictures. Tane hoped he could get a minute with his uncle, but it seemed his uncle took his pictures with the bride and groom and the family photo and disappeared. Tane knew this wasn't the time, or the place to get into what his uncle knew, but the more time that passed, his sin would eat at him. It wasn't having sex with Bailey that particularly worried Tane. It was that he received knowing he shouldn't have, that bothered him.

It seemed like the pictures took longer than the wedding did. But Lauren, the photographer that she was, wanted so many more pictures taken than the normal bride. Tane found himself once again feeling as if he had to bide his time.

Everyone sat in different pews waiting to be done. Tane took this time to kneel and confess to God himself. *Forgive me, Lord, for I have sinned against you. I took communion knowingly that I was not worthy of your body and blood. I had sexual intercourse with Bailey knowing it was a sin. Defying your wishes. I have no excuse except that I'm human and I failed you. I even went to the extreme of sinning against you in your house. I ask for your forgiveness, and mercy on my soul, in Jesus' name, I pray.* Tane knew there would be no absolution for him until he confessed to a priest. But if he had any relationship with God, he hoped his request was heard. Tane sat back in his seat, and no one seemed to notice him praying, except for Bailey who was sitting on the other side of the church.

When it was time to head to the big hotel where the reception was to be held, everyone piled into the limos. Lauren's father didn't scrimp on anything for his only daughter's wedding.

Bailey managed to catch up with Tane so they could sit next to each other on the ride. They didn't say anything to one another because there were so many people in the car that could overhear them. Bailey slipped her hand under his arm to show him her support. She had a feeling Tane was starting to feel guilty about having sex with her and hoped he wouldn't withdraw from her. But there was a good possibility he would, and she tried to prepare herself for that. Having sex with someone always seemed to complicate things.

As they went inside the hotel, Bailey looked for signs that Tane would break things off with her. They all went into a big room with food and drinks for the bridal party to wait until the cocktail hour was over and they would be introduced to Paul and Lauren's guests in the grand ballroom.

Tane stood in the back. This kind of stuff made him feel uncomfortable. It was a social gathering, and he was an introvert. Bailey smiled at him, and he nudged his head for her to come. They stood close but not too close. He said, "I hate these things."

"Is that why you're standing way over here?"

"Yes. I'd go home if I thought I could get away with it."

"That's terrible. This is your brother's wedding. You should be having a good time." Bailey looked up at Tane, "Do you know how to have a good time?"

"What I call a good time and what other people's definition of a good time are two different things."

"What would you consider a good time?"

"Being alone with you."

Bailey smiled up at him and then became serious, "I thought when I saw you in the church…you might be feeling guilty."

Tane glanced down at her, "Oh, I am. But I wouldn't change it. I did things that I knew were wrong. Let me rephrase, I did it out of order."

"Let's go, time to party!"

Tane and Bailey lined up because they were always first to be announced. He looked at it as more time that he could touch Bailey without drawing anyone's attention. Once their names were announced Tane and Bailey moved to the center of the dance floor. Bailey had her arm around Tane's. As each couple were announced, they too stood waiting for the bride and groom to be formally introduced. Tane watched as his brother spun Lauren into his arms. Paul never looked happier than he did right now.

Bailey whispered, "Did you see Paul crying as he watched Lauren walk down the aisle? I want that kind of love."

Tane didn't think Bailey realized what she said to him. It was more like she was thinking out loud. He took her in his arms as everyone joined the happy couple. "Have you ever thought about your wedding day?" Tane was sure to pull Bailey in a little tighter than he would have before.

Bailey laughed, "Like when I was little, but nothing serious. I'm in high school. What do I know about a real relationship? I've had a few boyfriends. What about you…oh, never mind. Sorry, I wasn't thinking." They danced around the floor and when the song was over, they went their separate ways as they agreed to do.

There were too many people in the bridal party to have a single head table, so all the bridesmaids and groomsmen sat at separate tables. There was no assigned seating, just what table you sat at. Tane, Bailey, Ava, Daniel, Patrick, Shana, Gabe, and Faith were sitting together. Bailey sat next to Faith, while Tane sat across from her, next to Ava. While everyone else filled the seats in between them.

Daniel asked Ava if she wanted something to drink. "I would like a soda. Thank you, Daniel." Once he got up to get her drink, Ava leaned into Tane, "How's things going? You and Bailey seem to be getting along."

Tane didn't want to get into any details with his sister, "We talked."

"That's good, right?"

Tane just shook his head, yes. He spotted his uncle and said, "I'll be right back." Tane said, "Uncle Joe, can I speak to you, privately?"

"Not now, Tane. I'm not here as a priest. I'm just the uncle of the groom. If you want to speak to me, make an appointment."

Tane was taken back by the way his uncle was brushing him off. "This is important. Please, Uncle Joe."

Joe moved out into the hall so they could talk freely. "What's so important?"

"I…I wanted to say, I'm sorry."

"Tane, what are you apologizing for?" When Tane didn't say anything, Joe said, "Here's what I know. Last night someone used the code to open the door to the Parish Hall after everyone left. I saw two figures move through the hall into the kitchen and disappear. Fifteen minutes later, a female reappeared going into the restroom. Then someone who looked very much like my nephew followed her. You need to make an appointment with me if you want to discuss this matter any further, or if you feel the need to make a confession. Now, I'm going back to the celebration."

Tane watched his uncle walk away from him and it hurt his chest to see his uncle so mad at him. Uncle Joe was the one person Tane always felt understood what he was going through. Now he was a sinner like everyone else. Tane never went back to the table. He found a quiet place to hide.

{11}

Bailey realized Tane had been gone a long time. The last time she saw him he was talking to his uncle, and she figured that didn't go well. So, she took it upon herself to find him because no one else would even realize he was missing. She asked if Tane was in the restroom. Bailey got some strange looks from the guys coming out of the bathroom, but Tane wasn't in there. As she moved through the hotel, she looked in every nook and cranny, her mind went to where she'd go to be alone. *The stairwell*! And that's right where she found Tane. He was sitting on the steps with his back leaning up against the wall.

"There you are. I was looking everywhere for you."

"Sorry, I couldn't take it and needed some time to myself."

"Does that include me?" She sat on the same stair as him.

"I'm not very good company right now. So, if you want to go. I'll understand."

Bailey put her hand on Tane's knee, "Why don't you tell me what's got you feeling this way?"

"I don't want to talk about it. I made my own mess."

Bailey had a good idea of what he was talking about. "We made this mess, Tane. We did this."

Tane shook his head, "No, Bailey. You don't understand. I knew better."

"Okay, we aren't perfect. Everyone makes mistakes. I'm…I know you…"

Tane said in a harsh tone, "You don't get it. I," he beat on his chest, "Am no better than anyone else. I'm a sinner and I will always be just that." Tane got up and walked out the side door that left the building.

Bailey didn't go after him because she didn't think anything she said would make him feel any better. "I don't know how to help you." She began to cry. After Bailey sat there for a long time knowing Tane wasn't coming back, she tried to pull herself together to go back to the wedding. If her and Tane both disappeared, everyone would think they were together. She slipped into a restroom away from the ballroom to clean her face. Once again Bailey tried to remove the dark rings around her eyes. "From now on, I have to wear waterproof mascara." She noticed this restroom had wet wipes instead of soap to wash your hands. Bailey grabbed one and began fixing her makeup. She took a deep breath and returned to the wedding.

Once Bailey entered the ballroom, she walked around so everyone could see her, but talked to no one. If someone asked her what was wrong, Bailey was afraid she'd fall apart. The one person she wanted to talk to was Tane's uncle. He had to say something to Tane to make him feel so bad about himself.

Bailey found Tane's uncle getting a drink by the bar. She gathered all her will and strolled up next to him. "Good evening, Father Joe. Are you enjoying the wedding?"

Joe glanced over at Bailey, "I am." He didn't add anything.

114

"I know you talked to Tane. I want to know what makes you the perfect person?"

"Excuse me?"

"You heard me. Haven't you ever made a mistake? Wait, I know you have because you judged Tane. You hold him up to a standard that no one can live up to. I hope you're happy living your perfect life. You, enjoy your evening now, Father Joe," Bailey turned and walked away. She was so mad, and found she couldn't stay any longer, looking at his perfect family. At least, they thought they were perfect. Bailey didn't even bother to tell her parents she was leaving.

Joe watched Bailey storm out of the room and then looked for Tane. He knew something was really wrong. Joe left his drink on the bar and searched for his nephew. Tane wasn't in the building and Joe left the wedding without alerting anyone. The first place he looked for Tane was at his house, he wasn't there. This was the city, Tane could be anywhere. Joe was feeling guilty for being so harsh with Tane. Yes, he was mad because Tane used a code to gain access to part of the church he had no right to be in and what they did in there.

Joe searched everywhere he could think. He even tried to call Tane with no answer. Joe went to the one place where he could think. When Father Joe opened the door to the church and saw Tane sitting in the front row, tears filled his eyes. Joe walked to the front of the church as he had done many times before, but this time he needed to be the uncle and not the priest. Joe said, "Is this seat taken?"

Tane looked up and shrugged as he moved over. "It's your church."

Joe sat and said, "I want you to know, I'm angry with you, but I need you to know I love you. And there isn't anything that will change that."

Tane leaned his head on his uncle's shoulder and began to cry. "I did something I can't take back. I will never be free of sin. You have every right to be angry with me, I knew better, and I defiled God's house. He will never forgive me."

Joe pulled Tane in close, "Listen my child. God knows your heart. You ask for his forgiveness and God will set you free. He knows we are not perfect because you see he gave us free will. We learn from our mistakes. Once you receive absolution, you are released from all your sins. The hard part is not repeating our wrongdoings. We all have sinned in some way."

Tane looked at his uncle, "You don't."

"Oh, yes. I'm not perfect. I know you may think I am," Joe shook his head. "I was called out by a little spitfire tonight. I did something I don't normally do. I judged. It's not my place to pass judgment. I am supposed to represent God, to help my parishioners or someone in need to find forgiveness or strength and mercy. You see, Tane we are not without our faults. That is why God forgives you if you are truly sorry."

"Uncle Joe, I'd like to confess my sins." Tane couldn't take the guilt any longer.

"Go ahead, my child." Joe took Tane's hand and closed his eyes.

"Forgive me Father for I have sinned. It has been two weeks since my last confession."

As Father Joe listened to Tane. He knew Tane had kept up his faith at school. Joe realized this was hard for his nephew, but a sin of this magnitude was difficult to overcome. Especially because Tane always held himself to a higher standard than most. Joe knew this particular sin well, the sin of pride. He too was at fault for expecting more from Tane.

"I took Bailey into the Parish Hall knowing full well what I was about to do was wrong. I love her, Uncle Joe. This wasn't just about the physical act. I thought if I went off to school it would be like my mother for you. You were able to go ahead with becoming a priest. I knew I had time and I hoped it would clear my mind of all thoughts of her. But no matter how hard I tried. They wouldn't go away. When I walked through the doors of the church and saw Bailey. It was like a force I couldn't control. I wanted her to know I was sorry for the way I treated her. I never hurt someone's feelings before, someone that I care so much about. Having sex with Bailey was more about a bond, something to tie us together. Not only did I have sex, but I did it in his house. How could I do such a thing? I understand you are mad at me because I deserve that, but you can't be any more disappointed in me than I am in myself." Tane stared forward looking up at the altar and Jesus Christ on the cross. He died to take away our sins. "Uncle Joe, why did you give me communion when you knew I didn't deserve to receive it?"

"Tane, I didn't know. I suspected something happened. I was hoping you'd make the right decision to not receive."

"I did it on autopilot. I took for granted that I never did anything so bad I couldn't receive the body of Christ. Everything I prided myself to be, was lost by one act."

"Tane, are you sorry? Ask God's forgiveness."

"Uncle Joe, I'm not sure I'm sorry. I should have handled this differently. But Bailey, and how I feel about her, I don't see that changing. I'm sorry we had sex out of wedlock. I'm sorry we did it on church grounds. I'm sorry I broke your trust in me."

"Then ask for absolution for the things you are sorry for, and you will have to live with the rest that you aren't. As I said, God knows what's in your heart."

After Tane said the Act of Contrition and Uncle Joe handed down Tane's penance, there was some relief even though his reparations were tough. Tane thought they were fair for what he did. There were several layers of his penance. Not only did he have to say prayers but had to serve in the church for abusing the trust of his uncle by using the code to enter the Parish Hall. When Tane returned from school for the winter break, he would have to be an altar boy and do other duties.

"Tane, I want you to know that serving in the church as part of your penance is me, hoping it will pull you back into the understanding of the church. You may not become a priest as you once thought, but you can serve God in so many ways."

"Uncle Joe, I am sorry for breaking your trust and I hope one day you can once again trust me. I hope you won't hold any of this against Bailey. She is not responsible for any of my indiscretions."

"I hope you know what you're getting yourself into with this young lady. She is the spitfire who called me out tonight. I believe this young lady has very strong feelings for you by the way she boldly defended you."

Tane frowned, "Bailey talked to you?"

"Oh, yes. She came right up to me at the wedding and asked what made me the perfect person. Then she went on to point out my faults, and I have to say, I was a little shocked and ashamed because she was right."

"That sounds like Bailey, bold, a little dramatic, and a whole lot tough when you get her mad."

"It sounds like you know her well. I would suggest you contact her to let her know you are alright. I know she's worried about you. Now, I will leave you to your prayers." Joe got up from the pew but didn't leave. "Tane, I don't want you to ever think I don't love you. You are a gift to us all."

Tane sat there thinking that he never felt like a gift to anyone. He was the last O'Shea child pulling up the rear. The one that no one paid attention to. It could be because that was the way he liked it. He could be a jerk like Gabe, or a bully like Paul to get attention. But he found being a hermit was easier than notching out a place in his family tree. There were too many bold, overbearing personalities. Take his sister Raylan for instance. She could come barreling in and be downright mean or be the best person to have on your side. Every one of them were O'Shea's but with so many different facets. There were the peacekeepers, like Ava, Grace, and even Patrick. His brothers Mack and Bryant were more like the leaders of the pack. Preparing their parents for the rest of the children that would come. He was just Tane, the youngest O'Shea.

Tane went to his knees a second time that day to ask God's forgiveness. He sure hoped God knew what was in his heart because Tane wasn't sure he knew himself.

Bailey ran up to her room as she pulled the bridesmaid's dress off her body. "I don't want to be in another O'Shea wedding. I don't care who it's for. I'm not doing it." She went into her bathroom to take a shower and get the stench of self-righteousness off her skin. "They think they are all so perfect, well they're not." Bailey stepped under the hot water and let the heat wash over her. "I don't know how Tane managed for this long without screaming. How dare they think they are better than everyone else." Bailey sighed, "And I thought he had it made." She turned so the water wet her hair. "I dreamt what it would be like to be in his big family. To have a sister to turn to or a brother to protect me. They are all self-centered people who only care about themselves. I'm so done with them." Bailey washed her body and got out of the shower. She knew she needed to call her mother to tell her that she had left the wedding.

Bailey was relieved when she got her mother's voicemail, "Mom, it's me. I left the wedding and I'm home. I didn't feel good and didn't want to draw attention away from the festivities. I love you." Bailey threw her phone on her bed and put on a tank and night shorts. She climbed into bed and closed her eyes when her phone went off. Bailey figured it was her mother and didn't answer it.

Tane left a message on Bailey's phone. He figured she was mad at him for once again walking away from her. "Boy, I'm just letting people down left and right." He left the church and went home. The house was dark, so he knew no one was there. Just the way he thought he liked it. Tane took off his suit and hung it up. He climbed into his bed and stared up at the ceiling. *How do I get Bailey to talk to me? I could call Ava and she could speak to Bailey.*

Tane grabbed his phone, "Ava, is Bailey right there?"

"Tane, where are you?"

"I went home…is Bailey there?"

"No, she's gone too."

"Thanks," Tane hung up as Ava still asked questions. He tried Bailey again and again. Each time he didn't wait for her voicemail.

"Tane, are you alright? I know I shouldn't have pushed you."

"Bailey, where are you?"

"I'm…home. Where are you?"

"I am too. I'm sorry for yelling at you. You did nothing wrong."

"I was worried about you. I knew you wouldn't answer my calls. I did something… you might not be happy about. I was so mad."

"You called out my uncle. He told me."

120

"Oh, God. What did he say?"

"He called you a spitfire and hoped I knew what I was getting myself into."

"I'm sorry, Tane. I just hate how you're treated. I'm pretty sure every one of your siblings has had sex before they were married and when you do it. Well, it's like you killed someone."

Tane laughed, "First, they didn't realize I have male urges. Secondly, they still see me as a kid and not an adult."

"I know, but they don't see you. Not the way I do, anyway."

"Bailey, I wanted to be invisible. Don't you see, it was easier for me."

"I understand what you're saying, but that still doesn't give them, all of them, the right to judge you."

"You're right, no one has the right to judge anyone else except God himself. Bailey, I have to return to school tomorrow. I won't have a lot of time before I leave. I might not be able to say goodbye in person."

"Tane, where do we go from here?"

"I will put in for a transfer on Monday morning. I don't know if I'll be able to get the classes I need for next semester because it's so late."

"And your parents, what will they say?"

"Bailey, I need to be honest about why I'm coming home."

"So, does this mean we are…boyfriend and girlfriend?"

"No Bailey, it means we are in a committed relationship."

"Oh. Tane, you told me you love me, but I didn't say it back."

"I know, and that's okay. I've walked away from you too many times. I'll wait until you see I'm not going anywhere."

"How long will you be gone?"

"I take semester finals before winter break, and then I'll be back the week before Thanksgiving."

"Wow, that's weeks away."

"I know, but it'll go fast, you'll see."

"I miss you already."

"Bailey, do you remember telling me I should gather all the information I could before making such a big decision?"

"Yes."

"I think you changed my course that day. I hoped I could go off to college and forget about you. But that didn't happen. It only made me miss you more."

"Good to know."

"You also said you'd bet that things would go beyond kissing."

"I didn't mean that as a challenge. I just knew if we kept hanging out and things got...you know. We would end up here."

"Did you notice how I didn't take on the bet? I may not have known it at the time. But I knew I sure liked kissing you."

"So, I guess it was a lucky thing you didn't take that bet."

"You don't bet on a losing hand."

"Tane, I never realized there were so many layers to you. You don't show very many people who you are. I wonder why you picked me."

"I know this is going to sound bad for me, but you were the first girl who showed enough interest in me for me to notice. And I want you to know, I hated that I noticed. But you never seemed to go away. Then you didn't even look at me. Not even one little glance and I…don't know. Something happened. I couldn't stop thinking about you. But I found no matter how embarrassed I felt to admit something, you never made me feel bad or weird. I could talk to you. The one person that I felt was on my side."

"I really wish you didn't have to go back to school so soon."

"I'll be back before you know it."

"Let me take you to the airport."

"Bailey, that's going to make leaving so much harder."

"I don't want my last memory of us being together where you yell at me and walk away. I would rather it be me kissing you at the airport. Even if I cry."

"Okay, but my dad was going to take me, so… I have to tell him."

"What time do I need to pick you up and what airport are you going to?"

Tane heard people moving around downstairs, "Look, I gotta go. Someone's home. I'll text you after I talk to my parents."

{12}

There was a knock on Tane's door. He pulled the covers over his lower half before he said, "Come in." It was his mother.

"I was wondering where you went. Ava said you went home. Are you alright?" Arlene went to put her hand on her son's forehead. "No one knew where you were, and then Ava said you called.

"I'm fine. I just had enough…of people. Bailey knew I left, and Uncle Joe knows too."

"Yes, well Bailey left, and your uncle disappeared too. Tane, did something happen between you and Bailey?"

Tane could see the concern on his mother's face, "Mom, I need to talk to you and Dad. Let me get dressed and come downstairs."

"Alright," Arlene went to the door and turned. "Tane, you know your father and I love you, right?"

Tane shook his head yes, "I'll be right down." He found his mother and father sitting on the couch waiting for him. "I don't mean to scare you, I'm okay. I don't want to continue my education…"

Arlene gasped, "You're quitting school?" Cadman held onto Arlene.

"No, I want to transfer. I want to come home. I don't think becoming a priest is in my future. This is a decision I didn't take lightly. I discussed this with Uncle Joe, and he understands, and suggested that I serve the church in a different capacity."

Cadman said, "Does this have to do with Bailey? Is she the reason you've decided not to become a priest?"

"I want you both to understand, that the decision was mine alone, but Bailey has become a very important part of my life. That's the reason I want to be closer to home. The moment I began to have doubts about what I wanted to do. I knew I had to look deeper inside myself. I don't want to disappoint anyone."

"Tane, this isn't about disappointing anyone. You must be true to yourself." Arlene stood and went to her son. She put her hands on Tane's face, "We will support you."

Cadman also stood, "Do you have any idea what you'd like to become? What field you'll be pursuing?"

"I'm not sure, but as Ava said, the first two years of college are getting your core classes done. I want you to know, I told Bailey I love her, and she wants to take me to the airport."

"Okay, son. I hope you know what you're doing."

"What did you say, Dad? You knew the minute you laid eyes on Mom and the kiss in the library sealed the deal. You and Mom were both younger than I am right now."

Cadman said, "Not by much."

"And I'm not getting married. I just want to date someone."

Arlene said, "I think it might be a little more than wanting to date."

Tane smiled as he stepped back toward the stairs and said, "We'll see." He disappeared up the stairs.

Arlene turned to Cadman, "There are far worse things than your son deciding not to become a priest."

"I'm a little surprised you aren't more concerned about this." Cadman looked into his wife's eyes. "You knew this would happen, didn't you?"

"I had a feeling. I know my children. I just hope they don't rush into anything now that he's made his decision clear."

"I'm having a hard time with him changing his mind after years of knowing what he wanted."

"Yes, what he thought he wanted. I thought I wanted to become a nurse and we all know how that turned out."

"You don't regret it, do you?"

Arlene pulled Cadman in close, "Not for one second. I love my life, our family, and most of all you."

Tane stood at the top of the stairs eavesdropping. He wanted to know how his parents really felt about what he told them. Tane took a deep breath and went to text Bailey.

The next morning Tane said goodbye to his mother and father. "I wish you could have stayed for Sunday dinner."

"Mom, I do too. You don't get the kind of meals you make here at school. But you knew this would be a fast trip." Arlene hugged Tane. His father stepped up to him and gave him a bear hug.

"We will see you after your finals. It will be good to have you home again." Cadman patted his son on the back.

Tane said, "I don't know. You and Mom have had the house all to yourselves for months now. I was hoping to stay the youngest."

Cadman looked at his son in shock. Tane was implying they were having sex and would have another child. Tane said, "I'm only kidding. But it was worth it to see the look on your face. Love ya, Dad." He walked off the porch to Bailey's car.

Cadman turned to his wife, "Who was that kid because he looks like our son, but he made a joke…a sex joke to boot."

"Tane just might prove to be our wildest child of them all."

Cadman shook his head, "No, I'm not sure I can take it. He was the easy kid."

Arlene stood on the porch and waved to her son, "I'm giving you fair warning," and smiled at the look on her husband's face as she went back inside.

The ride to the airport wasn't long. Bailey wanted to say so many things to Tane. But was afraid the minute she opened her mouth she'd start crying. Tane asked, "You're awfully quiet. Is everything alright?"

"I'm trying to maintain my composure," she glanced over at him sitting in the passenger seat. "I don't need to be driving with tears running down my face."

"Ah, Bailey. I knew this was going to be too hard. I should have let my dad bring me. I don't want you crying."

"I'll do my best, but I won't make any promises." Bailey pulled into the short-term parking and didn't move to get out.

Tane said, "I will miss you."

Bailey took deep cleansing breaths. "I can do this. You've been gone for months, and I managed."

"You were mad at me."

"You broke up with me."

"Technically, I didn't. You thought I was breaking up with you and broke up with me before I could say anything."

"Are we going to argue here, before you leave?" Bailey turned to see a smile on Tane's face. "What are you smiling at?"

"You won't cry if you're mad."

"You wanna bet? I cried plenty while I was mad at you."

"I'm sorry," he leaned over and kissed the grouchy look off her face. "Is that better?"

"I guess, you might need to try again to be sure."

Tane grinned, "Okay, now you're getting greedy."

"Forget it. No more kisses for you." Bailey got out of the car.

Tane followed her, "You know I was only kidding." He took her hand as they entered the airport.

"It's a good thing you're cute." She put her chin in the air. They both knew they were avoiding talking about him leaving. Bailey walked with Tane as far as she could. She put her arms around his waist, and he took her face in his hands to make her look up at him. "I love you. We will talk every day, video chat." Tane leaned down and kissed Bailey. He didn't care who saw them.

"I'll be counting down the days." They kissed one more time and Tane detangled himself from her and went into the security line. He looked back and Bailey covered her mouth as she did her best not to cry. She stood there until she couldn't see him anymore. Her phone dinged, a message from him saying he missed her already. She put a kissy face and said, back atcha. Tane would call her when he landed.

Bailey walked back to her car and got in line to exit the airport. Her phone rang and she was hoping it was Tane, but she didn't recognize the number, so she didn't answer it. Once she got on the highway to head home, her phone chimed to let her know she had a voicemail. "That will have to wait." She knew it wasn't Tane so it couldn't be important. When Bailey got home, she listened to the voicemail.

"Hi, Bailey. This is Arlene O'Shea. I'd like to invite you to Sunday dinner. I understand this is short notice, but we would love to have you. We hope to see you. Oh, and dinner is at three-thirty. Bye."

Bailey didn't know what to do about that. She was still mad at Tane's family for being such jerks. Plus, she didn't want to go without him, it would be just weird. She could see herself sitting at their table with everyone looking at her and wondering what she was doing there. *No, thank you.*

Bailey decided not to do anything. She'd wait to talk to Tane first. But she was pretty sure eventually she'd have to speak to Arlene. His mother didn't seem like a person to give up so easily. Bailey knew it would take Tane a while from the time his fight took off and landed before he'd call her. "There should be plenty of time to call Mrs. O'Shea to decline her offer for dinner."

Tane looked out the window as his plane took off. He hated to have to leave so soon after getting back with Bailey. They didn't even get to spend that much time together. He knew that was his fault. Pulling Bailey into the Parish Hall was wrong on so many levels, but was he sorry they shared that closeness? Nope. It meant something to him. Bailey never admitted that she had sex before, but he knew she did. Tane hoped she felt what they did was more than just sex because it sure was to him. Once he moved home, Tane knew he needed to have a tighter grip on physical stuff. You can't ask forgiveness and continue to repeat the offense. The next time they come together, she would be his wife.

Tane knew this time away from each other would only make their relationship stronger. It sure made his feelings for her deeper. Tane closed his eyes to think about when he first saw her in the front of the church. How his body craved her, and he was reminded how badly he screwed up. But each time, Bailey forgave him and took him back. Now, he knew what he wanted. It was no longer a guessing game. As Tane sat there he let the scene in the pantry play through his mind. It was dark but he sure could picture what Bailey looked like in her bra and panties. When she pulled her dress over her head, he knew what she had under it. The day when they went to the baseball game, he saw her moving around in her bathroom. So, he pictured her in that light pink bra and thong. Tane's body started to react to his visual replay.

"Sir, would you like something to drink? A snack perhaps?"

Tane folded his hands in his lap and said, "No, thank you." He'd save his sex replays for when he was in his bed, alone. Tane looked out the window again and thought, *I should have never decided to go to school so far away.*

You know why you did. You needed to get out from under your crushing family and grow into the person you wanted to be.

That's not true. I just needed some of my own space.

Isn't that the same thing?

I didn't know being alone could be terrible. I liked being by myself because I knew my family was always there. Tane took out his headphones. He didn't want to hear his own thoughts and he definitely couldn't close his eyes.

Tane was never so happy for the plane to land, and he could take his phone off airplane mode. He got off the plane with the same overnight bag. Tane stood in the airport and called Bailey. She answered on the first ring as if she was waiting for his call.

"You made it."

"Yes, I made it, safe and sound."

"Good, I have to talk to you about something."

"What could have happened in the short time I've been gone?"

"Your mother called me and invited me to dinner. What do I do?"

"When?"

"Today, like two minutes after I left the airport."

"No, when did she invite you for dinner? What day?"

"Today, that's what I'm trying to tell you. Your mother invited me to Sunday dinner with your entire family."

"Well, not all. Paul and Lauren won't be there."

"Tane… what should I do?"

"Go if you want to go and don't if you don't want to."

"That is not helpful. I don't want to go and have everyone looking at me and wondering why I'm there. What do I tell your mother? Or better yet, why don't you call your mother and tell her I can't come?" Bailey heard Tane laugh on the other end, and it made her smile. "Tane help me. I'm still kinda mad at your family for the way they treat you."

"Bailey, don't be mad at them, it's a waste of energy. Listen, be honest, and tell my mother you feel uncomfortable. She can't force you to go."

"She will continue to try and make me feel comfortable. I will not go until you go with me. End of discussion."

"Fine, so it's settled. What are you doing?"

"What? Um…I'm sitting on my bed. What are you doing?"

"I'm standing in the airport."

"I miss you."

"I miss you too. What is a good time to call you tomorrow?"

"Uh…I get home after the salon around six-thirty."

"I have to go and get back to my dorm. I have a few papers to turn in."

"On Sunday?"

"In college, you turn in papers electronically. They're due before tomorrow so one minute after midnight, it's considered late. Bailey, I love you, and I'll call you tomorrow."

"Bye, Tane."

Bailey felt a little sad. She wouldn't see Tane for weeks. He would miss her eighteenth birthday. "I bet he doesn't even know when my birthday is. I certainly don't know his." But she was a whole lot happier inside. Tane said they were in a committed relationship. Not that she really knew what that meant because she'd never been with someone as mature as Tane. That was a funny thought because Tane was more mature than most, but he was also very inexperienced with relationships. She was his first girlfriend.

A little nagging feeling came over her, what if he realizes that other women may be attracted to him? Tane may feel more confident now that he had sex with her. *His trial run.* Bailey shook that thought off. Tane wouldn't do that to her. He didn't look twice at her co-worker at the ice cream shop. She told herself, *I'm just making things up in my head. Tane loves me. I have to trust in that. Besides, there are no girls at his school, so there's nothing to worry about. He will call you tomorrow and we will talk every day. The time will fly by, as he said. Plus, I have a lot going on to keep busy. Now, to deal with Tane's mother. Oh, God, I do not want to do this.*

Bailey hit redial and Arlene's phone rang. *What do I say, what do I say?* "Mrs. O'Shea, it's Bailey. I got your message."

"Oh, good. I hope you will be able to join us for dinner."

"I'm sorry, but I won't be able to make it. I have…schoolwork to finish. With the wedding and all."

"Oh, I understand. Maybe next week perhaps?"

"Mrs. O'Shea, I don't feel comfortable. I would feel out of place."

"Bailey now that you and Tane are together, I was hoping we could get to know you."

"He told you…we were together?"

"Are you not together? Have I misunderstood? I'm sorry if I…"

"Oh, no, Mrs. O'Shea. Tane and I are together. But it's new and we just kinda got back together and now he's gone." Bailey thought why not put it all out there so Arlene knew exactly why she didn't want to sit at her table. "Mrs. O'Shea, your family has only been nice to me, but if I'm being truthful. I don't like how Tane is treated. He left the wedding really upset and I'm sure no one noticed. Your family treats Tane as if he's invisible. No one except me went to look for him. If you don't mind me asking, when did you notice Tane was gone?"

Arlene was shocked by Bailey's accusation. "Yesterday was a busy day for everyone," she tried to keep her composure. "Tane is an adult and had the right to leave without telling anyone. I wasn't happy to hear from Ava that Tane left the wedding. As you know, getting my son to express his feelings is difficult, to say the least. I do resent you implying we don't care about Tane."

"Mrs. O'Shea, I mean no disrespect. I wasn't implying you don't love Tane. But I've been thrown in with Tane for many events now, and I do understand his lack of social skills or his need to separate himself from everyone else. But I would think that would make you keep a closer eye on him even more. I mean everyone, not you, in particular, Ma'am."

"Bailey, I think we should have tea sometime. Where we could discuss this matter further."

"Tea, Mrs. O'Shea?"

"Yes, when are you free?"

"Uh...I'm not sure."

"How about we plan for next Saturday?"

"Saturday?"

"Yes, it will be just you and me."

Bailey heard herself say, "Okay."

"Wonderful, I will see you on Saturday."

When Bailey hung up, she wasn't sure what happened. First, she was declining the invitation for Sunday dinner, and the next thing she knew she was agreeing to have "Tea" with Tane's mother. "Oh, she's good, really good."

{13}

Bailey rushed home after she got off from the salon. She didn't want to be driving when Tane called. Bailey ran up to her room. When her phone rang, she sounded out of breath. "Hello."

"Hello, yourself. Wow, you're breathless."

"Yeah, well, if you ran up two flights of stairs, you'd be out of breath too."

Tane laughed, "Why did you run up the stairs?"

"I wanted to be in my room when you called. I don't want anyone overhearing us."

"Oh, you still haven't told your parents about us."

"It's bad enough, your parents know. I don't need to throw a monkey wrench into the mix. I'm having "Tea" with your mother on Saturday. So, we can discuss you. Fun, huh?"

Tane laughed again, "You know, my mother won't bite you. You're someone important to me, and she just wants to get to know you better."

"Well, it might have more to do with what I said to her."

"Bailey, what did you say?"

"You told me to be honest," Bailey held her breath waiting for what Tane would say.

"What did you say?"

"I declined your mother's offer for dinner with the excuse I had homework to do. Which, I did, but I also said I felt uncomfortable."

"And."

"And, I might have said I didn't like the way your family treats you. I asked your mother when she noticed you were gone last night."

"Aww, Bailey. You don't have to fight my battles. I've been in this family a long time."

"And, yet you never said anything, shocker."

"I liked flying under the radar. It meant I could do what I wanted without anyone making a big deal out of it. Did you ever think my mother gave me the room to withdraw when I felt overwhelmed?"

"Fine that's fair, but what happens when you aren't just withdrawing? What if you are in trouble or upset? What good is having a big family like yours if you can't turn to any of them? None of them went looking for you."

"That's true, but I never had problems until I met you. Hear me out. I didn't know how to handle my feelings for you. I certainly didn't understand them."

"I would hope if you went to Mack or Bryant they would talk to you, guide you. Help you understand what you were going through. They're guys. Don't guys stick together?"

"I never asked for help because I didn't feel the need. Before you, of course. Bailey, I didn't want anyone to know how I was feeling, much less what I was thinking because I felt guilty and weak. I was becoming a priest that was having sexual thoughts about you. I

136

didn't want anyone to know. I talked to my uncle, but it didn't help. He never had… or never admitted to having those kinds of thoughts. He was trying to help me stay on the path to becoming a priest because that's what he thought I wanted. At a time when that path was taking a sharp left. I did talk to Ava."

"Ava? Really? I wouldn't have guessed she'd be the one you'd turn to, but what do I know. I don't have anyone."

"Bailey, it's me who has to learn to ask for help when I need it. If I truly needed anyone in my family, they would be there for me. I know they would, I've seen it. So, don't be mad on my account."

"Okay, but you aren't invisible. I won't let you be."

"We make a great team. What they say about opposites attract is true."

"Tane, if you were with another introvert, you would never talk."

Tane laughed, "I think I've talked more since that day you rang the doorbell, than I have in all of my nineteen years."

"Oh, when's your birthday?"

"That's random. It's November third. When's yours?"

"It's actually coming up. I turn eighteen on October twelfth. I hate that you couldn't be here to celebrate it with me. My parents talked about having a party, but I don't think I want to do that. Not without you."

"We can celebrate both of our birthdays when I come home. So, tell me about your day." Tane liked it when Bailey filled the air with her chatter. She always had an upbeat way about her, except for when she was battling his family on his behalf, then she was fierce. Tane stretched out on his bed and listened to her tell him about all the haircuts she did. He didn't need to say a word.

On Saturday, Bailey made her way to the O'Shea house. She kept telling herself she could leave at any time. *I can just get up and walk out.* Bailey stood at the front door as she took a deep breath. The last time she stood here, Tane answered the door without a shirt. "You won't be so lucky today." Bailey pushed the bell and stood back.

"Bailey, I'm so glad to see you. Please come in." Arlene opened the door wider for Bailey to move inside.

"Hi, Mrs. O'Shea."

"Bailey, everyone usually uses the side entrance." She closed the front door and moved down the hall to the kitchen.

Bailey looked around, "Where is everyone? The house is so quiet."

"Oh, the house is quite calm these days. Cadman is working and with Tane gone, most days it's just me." Arlene filled the teapot full of water. "I'm sorry, I didn't ask, do you drink Tea?"

"Um, not really, but I'll have some." Bailey thought, *can you put a shot of whiskey in it?*

"I think drinking tea calms your nerves." Arlene turned to see Bailey standing in the doorway of the kitchen. It looked as if she was about to make a run for it. "Please have a seat," she put out her arm.

Bailey moved to sit against the wall. She figured Tane's mother didn't sit there. "Mrs. O'Shea, about the last time we spoke. I was out of line. I don't understand the dynamics of a big family."

The teapot began to whistle, and Arlene took it off the stove. She pulled two cups from the cupboard and put tea bags in each. "You might not know how things are in a big family, but I do respect your perspective." Arlene put the cup in front of Bailey, and she sat at the end of the table next to her. "I wasn't completely shocked when Tane came to us about his decision not to become a priest. You see, I've seen Tane and how he acted around you. What I didn't realize

138

was just how much he was struggling. There are times to step in and others, you must hold your ground no matter how much you want to help. Children need to learn to solve their own problems. I know you may not agree, but it's how they grow. If I went to look for my son, he wouldn't have told me what was bothering him, not that I didn't know something was going on when the two of you didn't return from the church."

Bailey looked at the dark liquid in her cup. "I just think, this time, Tane really needed help. I couldn't make him feel better and when he left. I was afraid he might…do something."

"Bailey, there are times we have to turn what weighs heavy on us to the Lord. We have to have faith that God will take care of us, and things happen for a reason. As it turns out, Tane ended up where he needed to be and got the help he needed from the right person."

"What you don't understand is Tane has never been on the sinning side of God. He held himself to a standard no one could uphold forever. Tane looks up to his uncle so much and when he tried to talk to him, Father Joe brushed him off. Tane felt as if he had no one to turn to. It broke my heart to see him suffering so much because of me and no one was helping him." Bailey wiped a tear from her eye. I was mad that no one seemed to notice how much Tane was hurting."

"Apparently, Tane has let you into a place where he keeps the rest of us at arm's length." Arlene put her hand over Bailey's, "I'm glad he has someone like you. Someone, that will speak your mind when need be because you'll need that in this family. Even I, every once in a while, need to be reminded. I may not like it, but no one is perfect. Not even my brother-in-law."

"Oh, I did say some harsh things to Father Joe." Bailey felt her face heat.

"The way I hear it, you were right. And you weren't wrong about keeping an eye on Tane." Arlene smiled, "But it's hard to keep your eye on nine children. You would think it gets easier as they become adults. Being a mother is a full-time job and you never retire. But the reward you get for your hard work is worth every sleepless night, and gray hair." Arlene smiled at Bailey.

"Thank you, Mrs. O'Shea. I was so afraid to come over here."

"I'm always open for discussion. Now, why don't you drink your tea before it gets cold and tell me how school's going."

The next two weeks passed, Tane and Bailey spoke on the phone. He liked when Bailey used her computer to video chat with him. Tane could see Bailey's cute little hairdos. One time she had her blonde hair in a big messy bun on top of her head. The next time she had two little knob-looking things. Tane asked her if she'd go back to her natural color. She said she would, for him.

Every time they had to hang up, sucked. It never felt long enough. Tane noticed that Bailey never brought up their little tryst in the Parish Hall. He was sure she didn't want to make him feel guilty. But it didn't stop him from thinking about it. Thoughts of her happened at the most inconvenient times. He could be in religion class or listening to a boring lecture. His mind would go right to her light pink bra and thong. Of course, the entire reenactment took up his nights.

Bailey called him all excited, "I'm doing my first fashion show."

"Okay, a fashion show? Am I supposed to know what that means?"

"I have to pick three models, one is formal, one is fantasy, and the last one is a bold stylish look."

"I still don't get it. What do you do with the models?"

"I pick their clothes, do their hair, and makeup. It's a competition. I will be competing against the other hairstylists from my school and other schools. We only have three hours to get everyone ready to walk down the runway."

"Wow, three hours? Do you think you can do it?"

Bailey sighed, "Give me some credit. The trick is to do as much as you can beforehand."

"Who are you going to get as models?"

"I have a few friends, but I don't know."

"I have three sisters you could ask. I see Ava doing it. Oh, and Faith too, maybe Shana. There are so many to choose from. My mom might even do it for you."

Bailey laughed, "I can just see your mom as my fantasy person."

"I'd save the formal or the bold chic for my mother, and have Faith do the fantasy. Wait, what kind of fantasy are we talking about?"

Bailey laughed, "Like Sci-fi, not what you see in your dreams."

Tane thought he'd have a little fun with Bailey. "That's all I have to keep me going." Bailey got quiet, "Am I embarrassing you?"

"Me? No. I'm just a little surprised, that's all."

"Why?"

"It's just a subject we don't talk about. I didn't think you wanted to be reminded that I was your biggest…sin."

"Aw, Bailey. It doesn't just go away. I'm not talking about just the sin but the thoughts and images I have of you in my head."

"I...ah...don't know what to say to that."

"That's a first. You... don't know what to say."

"I think I started my period, if that's any consolation?"

"You think? I'm not going to pretend I know anything about that stuff."

"Well, my cycle isn't regular, meaning I don't always get it when I should and sometimes it's more than others."

"Okay, so you're not pregnant?"

"No. I'm not." Bailey heard Tane sigh. "Anyway, I think the fashion show should be fun."

Tane noticed how Bailey changed the subject. "Yeah, you got this. When is it?"

"Thanks, it's in three weeks."

"I'm sorry, I'll miss it."

"I have to do three of them before I graduate, so you can catch the next one."

"I'll be there cheering you on."

"I can't see you drawing any kind of attention to yourself."

Tane laughed, "That was the old me. Now, I have to support my better half the way she's always my cheerleader."

"We'll see. I have homework to do and I'm starving. Will you call me tomorrow?"

"Wouldn't miss it. Bailey, I love you."

"Me too. I'll talk to you tomorrow."

Tane hung up and smiled. Bailey said me too, as in she loved him too. She was coming around. He thought about Bailey not being pregnant. It was a good thing. They were just getting to a good place. Tane couldn't wait to leave school so he could be with Bailey to go on dates and have some fun together. It would be a blessing and a curse. He'd be happy to have Bailey in his arms again, but having her so close would invoke those strong physical needs. "I have to just control them." He couldn't let things get that far.

The next two weeks passed, and Bailey's birthday came. Tane texted her, wishing her a happy birthday. She went to school as if it was any other day. Her friends sang to her during lunch before she went to school at the career center. There, she was presented with a tiara. It had fake diamonds with an eighteen in the center. Bailey wore it all night and made great tips from her customers. She couldn't wait to get home so she could talk to Tane.

When Bailey walked through the door of her house. Her parents wanted to take her out for dinner. "Just give me a minute to change."

Louisa came to the bottom of the stairs, "Bailey, this came for you in the mail today."

Bailey walked down to take it. "Thank you, Louisa." She didn't remember ordering anything. As she walked up the two flights of stairs to her room, she noticed the return address. The package was from Tane. Bailey figured she was out of earshot from her parents and she called Tane.

"Hey, I got your box."

"Happy birthday. Do you like it?"

"I haven't opened it yet."

"Oh, hang up and video chat with me, so I can watch you open it." Tane didn't wait for her to respond, he hung up and went to his computer. He opened the video app and Bailey's image popped up.

She looked so cute with a tiara on her head, and he noticed she changed her hair color back. Tane smiled. "Okay, make sure I can see you open it. Bailey got a pair of scissors and sliced the tape holding the box closed.

"I don't have long because my parents want to take me out to dinner." Bailey pulled out a cute teddy bear that said 'I love you" on his chest. Bailey hugged the soft bear. "I love it. Thank you, Tane."

"I thought you'd sleep with it and think of me. Where did you get the cute tiara? It suits you."

Bailey reached to touch the crown on her head as if she forgot it was there, "Oh, it's something they do at school. I mean in the salon."

"Leave it on. I like it. I wish I'd thought of it."

"I love my bear. He will be your stand-in until you get home."

Tane watched as Bailey pressed the bear to her chest. "I'm jealous."

Bailey heard her mother calling her, "My mom is calling, I need to get changed."

"Okay, call me when you get back." Tane hated that he couldn't be there with her.

"We can still talk while I change." Bailey went into her closet and came out with other clothes in her hand. "Tell me what's going on with you." She stood on the other side of the room and took her T-shirt and pants off.

Tane leaned in to watch her. Bailey moved quickly, so he didn't get to see much as he knew it was her intent. "I took a few...ah...tests. Nothing exciting."

Bailey moved into view, "I'm sorry. I have to go. I'll call you when I get back and we can talk more."

"I love you."

"Me too." Bailey kissed her screen and then disconnected.

Tane sat there a long time after Bailey was gone. "Holy shit." He wished he could have recorded their conversation so he could replay it in slow motion and maybe zoom in. It wasn't what he could see as much as what he wanted to be able to see. Tane knew it would be wrong to ask Bailey to show herself to him. But that didn't stop him from thinking about it.

{14}

The following week Bailey was busy with the fashion show. She asked Faith, Ava, and Shana to be her models. The Sunday before the show everyone met up at Bailey's house after church. She had five days to get her act together. Bailey picked Ava to be her formal model. Shana was going to be her bold chic, and Faith her fantasy.

Ava was first. She held up an old, crocheted wedding dress. "Ava, I love this dress." Bailey looked it over. The dress had a cross crocheted along the back of the train. It was a little yellowed, but Bailey thought that added to the charm.

"I had to have it when I found it in the thrift store. I was hoping Ray or my mother could make it into a real wedding dress for me."

"Oh, then you don't want to wear it for this. What if something happened to it?"

Ava smiled, "Then I wasn't meant to have it. But it doesn't have a lining and I can't wear it like this."

"Wait, let me see what I can come up with." Bailey went into her closet and came out with a cami and cream-colored fitted pants. "Try these on with the dress. You can use my bathroom." Bailey looked at Shana, "Now let's see what you brought." Shana held up a suit

146

jacket and a pair of slacks. "Okay, let's see. Can we change things up?"

Shana asked, "What did you have in mind?"

"Can I...hmm."

"You can do whatever you want. I was getting rid of these clothes anyway."

"Wonderful. I want to cut off a leg and sleeve from each. What do you think?"

Faith asked, "On the same side or opposite?" She stood next to Bailey.

Ava came out of the bathroom, and everyone turned to look at her. "Wow, Ava. That dress looks like it was made for you." Bailey walked over to her. "I see an updo with pearls in your hair." She twisted Ava's long strawberry-blonde hair up and held it. "What do you guys think?"

"Shana said, "Make her into the traditional Irish bride."

Faith agreed, "Yes."

Bailey pulled down some strands, "I could make these ringlet curls, with a braided headdress. Wait, what do you think if we do all ringlets with...no, I got it. Bailey loosely braided Ava's hair. "I can add flowers and pearls."

Faith asked, "That sounds great, but can you do her hair and the rest of us in three hours?"

"Don't forget makeup," Bailey said as she still was looking at Ava.

Shana asked, "What do you see for me?"

Bailey turned her attention to Shana and said, "A mohawk. We will make your hair stand right up."

Shana said, "Cool. One question. Will you have to shave the sides of my head?"

"I don't have to." Bailey went to her. "We can clip it up," Bailey pulled Shana's hair to the center of her head. "Then make it stand up from there. Maybe even spikes."

Faith asked, "So, what are you going to do for me?"

"Now, Faith, I want to color your hair purple. I mean really purple."

"Sounds good. Now what am I going to wear?" Faith rubbed her hands together.

"Here's what I have in mind for you." Bailey went into detail laying out what Faith would wear and how she planned to do her makeup. Faith would take up most of Bailey's time. But if she did things right, she could get it all done. Once the plan was set it was time for Ava, Faith, and Shana to head to the O'Shea's for Sunday dinner. Bailey still hadn't gone.

Faith took Bailey's hand, "Come to dinner with us. I know Arlene made plenty. Plus, it would make her really happy."

Bailey looked over at Tane's sister, and Ava said, "I promise we don't bite."

Bailey took a deep breath, "I just don't want to feel out of place."

Shana said, "Join the club. We all feel out of place. So, we'll stick together." They convinced Bailey to go.

When the girls walked through the side door of the O'Shea house, Arlene was surprised to see Bailey with them. She didn't want to make a fuss and draw attention to the fact. Arlene greeted everyone. "Welcome, you are just in time. Ava, will you please set the table and the girls can help you?"

Bailey glanced over at Tane's mother by the stove as she waited for Ava to hand her what she'd be putting out on the table. Bailey saw a little grin on Arlene's face as she stirred something in a pot. Bailey really wanted her first Sunday dinner to be with Tane so his family would know they were together, and she wasn't just crashing dinner. Ava handed her a wad of silverware and Bailey had to focus on what she was doing and not drop them.

As Ava put down the first plate at the end of the table closest to the kitchen, she said to Bailey, "This is where my mother sits." Ava pointed to the chair to the right. "That's where Tane normally sits, so you'll sit there. Unless, you'd rather sit somewhere else.

Bailey looked behind her at Faith. "Um, where do you sit?"

Faith smiled, "I sit over there," she pointed to the same side of the table but further down. "Next to Gabe."

Bailey then looked at Shana and she said, "I'll sit next to them."

"So, I'll be sitting next to you?"

Shana replied, "Well, you'd be next to Patrick. We sit boy, girl, boy, girl."

"Oh, couples," Bailey sighed, "Okay. I don't want to make a big deal out of this and have everyone notice they're sitting somewhere else. I'll just take Tane's chair." Ava smiled and continued down the table announcing where everyone would sit. It gave Bailey an idea of where everyone would be. It wasn't like she was on bad terms with Tane's mother. The last time they were together, they cleared the air.

When Cadman came in the door Arlene went to him, "Bailey's here, please don't make a big deal out of it. I don't want to scare her off."

Cadman said, "Me, make a big deal? Besides, I don't think that girl scares easily. She'll be around. Now, what do you need me to do, my love?"

Arlene smiled, "I could use a kiss." Just as their lips touched the side door opened, and Raylan, Jon, and the girls came in.

"Sorry, we're late. The girls were napping, and I didn't want to wake them." Arlene took the car seat out of her daughter's hand so she could take off her coat and shoes. Cadman took the other one from Jon. He placed the seat on top of the kitchen table.

Cadman cooed, "There's by Baby Girl."

Ray said, "Hey, I'm your Baby Girl."

Cadman turned, "You're all my Baby Girls." His attention went back to the baby in the car seat, as Arlene placed the other seat on the table. "Isn't that right, girls?" Both babies smiled and cooed back to him.

Arlene sighed, "Your father has always had a way with the females."

"Now, that's not true. There was only one female I had my sights on, and that was you, and the rest are my girls." He pointed to himself.

Ray went to her father, "And we love being your girls." She went on her tippy toes to kiss her father's cheek.

Jon said, "We know you love your daddy, Princess. Just like I want my girls to love me." He took both seats off the kitchen table.

"My dad sets the bar high."

Jon said, "Your dad is a great example of what a father should be."

"Oh, now you are just going to inflate his head." Arlene smiled as she went back to getting dinner ready.

Cadman put his arms around his wife's waist and said into her ear, "You're just jealous because they aren't talking about you."

"Oh, there's no mom better than ours," Ray said as she followed her husband out of the room.

Arlene said to Cadman, "Now she says that, but when the kids were growing up, I'm sure their opinions of me were completely different."

"Yeah, because you caught them doing all the things kids do. You are the soul of this family."

"And you are the heart."

The side door opened again and that was the end of the peace and quiet. It wasn't long before dinner was on the table, and they said, Grace. Bailey sat in Tane's chair, and no one looked her way or asked why she was there. Faith and Ava started talking about the fashion show. Ray asked, "What fashion show?"

Ava said, "Bailey has to do it for school. She's doing our hair and makeup. Plus, our clothes."

"Cool, I want to come. When is it?"

Shana answered, "It's this Friday."

Arlene asked, "This is for the career center, right? I'd love to go too."

Bailey watched as her one little event turned into a big deal. "Yes, I had to pick three models, Ava, Faith, and Shana agreed to do it. Each one is in a category. I will be judged for their makeup, hairstyle, and how they present in each group."

Ray said, "So, it's a competition. I do love a battle."

Grace asked, "What do you win?"

"We get money to spend at several beauty supply stores. They helped sponsor the competition. I probably won't win. There are a lot of schools and people who will be there."

Grace said, "I want to go, this sounds like fun."

Faith added, "I think you have a good shot to win something. Bailey only has three hours to make it all happen. Oh, I have a pair of old boots I could paint purple. If that would help."

Patrick asked, "What are the categories?"

"There's formal, bold-chic, and fantasy. Ava is my formal model, Shana is my Bold-chic, and Faith is fantasy."

Macy asked, "Do you have everything picked out, like what they're going to wear?

"That's the key, you have to have as much prepared as you can."

"Bailey, why didn't I know you were doing this? I want to go and support you."

"Aunt Julia, I didn't think you'd want to sit in a big, huge hall and watch hundreds of girls walk down a runway for hours. I only have three people that will take all of five minutes. I don't even know when my models will walk. They don't give us the number until we get there." Bailey looked around the table, "You could be there for hours, so I understand if you want to back out."

Lauren said, "I think it sounds like a great girl's night. I'd love to take pictures. I think it would be cool."

Gabe said, "So, Faith is fantasy. What kind of outfit is she wearing?"

"Fantasy as in Sci-Fi. I plan to make her a purple superhero, of sorts. I don't want to give too much away."

"I think the guys should go," Patrick said.

"Ah, you have to pay to get in. I really don't think everyone wants to sit and watch…"

Arlene put her hand over Bailey's, "I think it's wonderful if they want to support you. Let them go if they want to go."

"Um, okay, but don't say I didn't warn you how boring it's going to be," talk went on about how she would do three models in three hours.

Arlene looked down the table at her husband and he smiled. The girls of the family just surrounded Bailey and pulled her into the O'Shea fold. Cadman gave Arlene a little wink.

When Bailey got home from having dinner at the O'Shea's house, she called Tane to tell him how his family all planned to come to the fashion show. "I can't believe it. One minute Faith and Ava were talking about the show, and before I knew it, everyone wanted to come."

"Bailey, I'm glad my family is embracing you. But be aware they are drawing you in."

"I know. I figured as much. I could tell how happy your mother was as she looked at your father and he winked at her."

"Oh, yeah. You're in. Not that you weren't kinda in before. But now you are under the protection of the family."

"We haven't even really told anyone we're together."

Tane laughed, "That's the other thing you should know. The O'Shea family can't keep a secret to save their lives. If one knows eventually, they all know."

"It sounds like this makes you happy?"

"Of course, it does. I don't want my family to hate my girlfriend. But you do have it easier than when one of my sisters brought home someone. My older brothers really gave them a hard time."

Bailey asked, "Even Jon? Didn't he like grow up in your house?"

"Especially, Jon. He had a bad reputation, actually along with my brother Paul. So, my brother didn't want Jon dating Ray. But, once Jon proved himself to Ray, well, you know how that goes. Ray gets what she wants."

"Luckily, I've only been on the good side of your sister."

"And that's the best place to be."

"I miss you. I wish you could come home for the weekend, like you did for the wedding, but spend all your time with me."

"I know, it won't be long, and I'll be home for good. Just a few short weeks. Uh, I wanted to talk to you about something."

"Uh oh, what did I do?"

"Well, it's about your birthday."

"Yeah, what about it?"

"When we were talking before you went out for dinner, and you um, changed clothes."

"Yeah."

"Did you know I could see you? Well briefly."

"Tane we've been intimate. I didn't think that was a problem. Unless…it was for you?"

Tane sighed, "You know I'm stuck here and you're there. Well…"

"Oh, I'm sorry. I didn't want to hang up, but I get it. I won't do it again."

"That wasn't quite where I was going with this discussion."

"Oh! You want…?"

"I'm not sure what I want. All I do know is I can't stop thinking about it. I think about you in your pink bra and thong more times than I want to admit."

Bailey smiled, "It's nice to know I turn you on."

"If you only really knew. Your image pops into my head a lot."

"So, tell me what you want?"

He questioned, "What I want?"

"Yeah, when those images pop into your mind, what do you want to do about it?"

"I want to be in a bed somewhere alone with you."

"Okay, that's a start. Then what?"

"Bailey."

"Yes, Tane."

"This isn't a good idea."

"Okay, so why did you bring it up?"

"I don't know. I want to see you and you know, but on the other hand, I don't think we should."

Bailey laughed, "You're between a rock and a hard place. I was going to help you relieve your discomfort."

"Unfortunately, I have to suffer. But what happens when I come home and let's say we're alone. Which I want very much. I want you to know that you drive me crazy. I normally would suffer in silence."

"I thought you never thought about…sex.?"

"Oh, I didn't before you. I meant if I had a problem. But this…I don't know."

"You keep saying that you don't know, and I don't know how to help you."

"Can you be less, ah, sexy?"

"I'm not sure how to do that. We're talking on the phone."

"How about less cute?"

"Nope."

Tane sighed, "I guess I need to find a way to deal with the fact that I have a sexy, cute, adorable girlfriend."

"Cute and adorable mean the same thing. You have to think of another adjective to describe me."

"How about loveable? Will that work?"

"I guess that will do. I hate to do this, but…"

"You have to go."

"I have a lot to do before the fashion show. I need to run to the beauty supply to get Faith's hair color and figure out what she's going to wear. I have to stop by the Halloween store to get some stuff for her face makeup."

"This is all for Faith? What are the other girls wearing?"

"Oh, I'm doing your sister as an Irish bride. She brought what she's going to wear. All I really need for Ava is what I'll be putting in her hair. I have everything else. Shana also brought an outfit. I just have to make some changes to it. I have all her hair stuff and makeup. This is going to be a busy week for me."

"Not too busy for me I hope?"

"We can video chat or I could put you on speakerphone while I work. But I plan to do a trial run with each of my models. Well, except for Faith. I will be making a cast of the side of her face for a partial mask."

"Wow, you will be busy. I thought they gave you only three hours to get everything done."

"I told you it's all about the prep. You get everything done that you can beforehand. Believe me, the makeup and hair will take all of the three hours. Faith alone will take up most of my time."

"What are you doing to Faith? I know she's the fantasy, right?"

"Yes, and I'm making her into a movie-type superhero. At least, that's what I hope it will look like."

"Wow, that's cool. I bet Faith loved that you picked her as the fantasy category?"

"Yes, Faith was the right person for it. But to be honest, I think each model I chose will do well in their category."

"Do you think you'll win?"

"Well, there is a lot of competition, but I plan to do my very best. Now, there are several ways to win. You can win overall, meaning, you have the best in all categories, duh. Then you can win best in a single category. There's also second to fifth place."

"I wish I could be there."

"That's okay. I know I'll be so nervous. I will call you when it's over."

"You better. I love you, Bailey."

"Me too." Bailey hung up and got her list to get all her supplies."

{15}

Bailey's week was full of preparing everything she needed for the fashion show. Faith came into the school salon so Bailey could color her hair. Bailey went to Ava's dorm to do a trial run on her hair, so she knew just how she wanted the flowers and how many she'd need. She also spent time with Shana doing her hair and makeup. There wasn't much time to breathe, much less anything else, but she still made time for Tane, even if it wasn't much.

Bailey talked to Tane as she hand-sewed Shana's outfit, bundled baby's breath, and attached them to clips for Ava's hair. Bailey even video-chatted with Tane while she made the mask for Faith's face, and stitched gems onto Faith's outfit.

By the time Thursday night came Bailey was exhausted. She thought she'd pass out the second her head hit the pillow, but she couldn't be that lucky. Even when she drifted off, she dreamt of the fashion show. *I'm not ready. That couldn't possibly have been three hours. I only have one model done.* Bailey finally fell asleep right before her alarm went off for school. She turned it off and rolled over. Only if her mother would let her take off from school. It wasn't like she'd fall behind. Bailey closed her eyes and was out.

"Bailey, you are going to be late for school!"

Bailey sighed, "Can I stay home today? I didn't sleep last night."

Her mother stood in Bailey's doorway, "I think if you're absent from school you can't participate in the fashion show."

"Awl, crap. Can I go in late?"

"I'm not sure how an hour and a half will help you. You only have a half day as it is."

"Fine," Bailey pulled back the covers, *suck it up, buttercup. I'll just sleep in class.* Bailey suffered through her classes, but her ass was dragging. Tane texted her to wish her good luck and she didn't even respond. At least she didn't have to go to the career center after school.

Bailey went directly to the Civic Center where the event was being held. She got in line to check in. Bailey wished she asked Faith to meet her earlier because she was carrying everything she needed. Some people had those little shopping carts with wheels. Bailey made a mental note to do that next time. She decided to pile everything on her makeup case on the floor and push it with her foot as she moved up.

Once Bailey made it to the front of the line, she was given her packet. She moved to the side and opened the envelope. It had the location of her workstation and the numbers that her models had to wear. Now, Bailey had an idea of when each person would walk the runway. Unfortunately, Ava, Shana, and Faith didn't walk all at the same time. They went by categories. Bailey took a deep breath, picking up her stuff, and went in search of her station.

Once Bailey found where she'd be working, she began to set up her stuff. Then she texted Ava, Shana, and Faith. Next Bailey returned Tane's text.

Bailey: Thanks. I think I'll need all the luck I can get. There were a LOT of people in line to sign in. I didn't sleep last night so my butt is dragging.

Bailey sat in her chair and closed her eyes, but she didn't dare fall asleep. She'd wake up and all her stuff would be gone. In her head, she went over everything she had to do. Bailey's phone went off and she pulled it from her back pocket.

Shana: I'm here where do I go?"

Bailey: I'm on the second level and my booth number is two-forty-eight.

Shana: On my way.

Bailey thought, *okay that's one. If someone else is running late, at least I can start on Shana. I really need Faith here.* Bailey stood and stepped out of the curtain so that when Shana came around, she would see her. Shana smiled when she saw Bailey.

Bailey was relieved that Shana had her clothes in her hand. "We're in here," Bailey held the curtain open for Shana."

Shana said, "Wow, there isn't much room in here." Each booth or workstation was closed in by curtains so no one could see what the other hairstylist was doing.

"I can't imagine how many people are in this competition. There are five levels to this building and stations going all the way around."

"That's a lot of people. What do you want me to do?"

"I can't do anything until two o'clock." Bailey's phone went off again. Thank God, it was Faith. She sent the same text to Faith as she did to Shana. "That's Faith, now all we need is Ava."

Shana looked at her phone, "Ava should be here soon. Her last class ended a little while ago."

Bailey put her hand on her stomach, "I feel sick."

"Did you eat anything today?"

Bailey thought, "I don't think I have."

Shana started typing on her phone. "There, Ava is on her way and is bringing you something to eat."

The curtain opened and Faith came in. "Let's get this party started."

"We can't," Bailey and Shana said in unison. "We have to wait until two." Bailey went to her counter and pulled the envelope off. "I have your numbers. You have to have this visible to the judges and it's the number you will be walking. I'm sorry Faith, your category is last. I wish you all could walk in order, but they didn't ask me what I thought." Bailey handed each of them a slip of paper.

"Can we at least get dressed? That's not you doing our hair or makeup," Faith smiled.

"Um, I don't see why not. I think you have to change in here. We can step out while each of you gets changed."

Faith waved her hand, "I don't care if you stay. Let me see what I'll be wearing."

Bailey went to her bag and pulled out a stretchy one-piece suit that would cover Faith's entire body. "Now, I plan to cut a hole for your face. I will be gluing it in place, so you have to be really careful when you use the bathroom once you're in it. Here is the mask part that we talked about. I will airbrush it to match the other side of your face."

Faith asked, "Wow, did you sew all these things on here, or did it come like this?"

Bailey sighed, "I did it. I was hoping to be able to glue them on. But that didn't work so well. Anyway, here is your belt and your gun."

Shana asked as she took the green gun from Bailey's hand, "Is that a Marvin the Martian ray gun?"

"I believe it is. I wanted something to stand out."

"I love Marvin the Martian. I'll buy it off of you after you're done with it."

Bailey said, "You can have it. After the night I'm about to put you through, it will be well deserved." Ava stepped into the curtain with a bag of food.

"I didn't know what you wanted, so I got a couple things."

Bailey took the bag, "I'm not sure I can eat but it sure smells good." She stuck a few french fries in her mouth. "Before it gets crazy. I want to thank you guys for doing this for me. I realize this is going to be a long day and night for you guys. I want to take everyone out to lunch after this is over." Faith wrapped her arms around Bailey and Shana and Ava did the same.

"We got you, Bailey. Now, let's make some magic." Faith let go to change her clothes. "Am I supposed to wear anything under this thing?" The stretchy outfit fit like a second skin.

Bailey put the bag of food down, "You wear whatever you're comfortable in." There wasn't much room for them to move around, everyone shifted to one side to give Faith a spot to change. "What time do you have?" Bailey knew the closer the time came to starting, the more nervous she'd get. "I plan to start with Shana because she walks first and then Ava, and then Faith. Now Ava, I will be using an airbrush with Faith, and I don't want any purple makeup on your dress. You might want to wait to change."

Ava shook her head, "Okay."

"What time is it?"

Shana said, "You have fifteen minutes until two."

162

"I got this," Bailey said. Her phone went off and she knew it had to be Tane.

Tane: Remember I'll be rooting for you, and you are tough and strong. Just get mad at it and I'm sure you will blow right through this. You can sleep after you've collected your prize money. Know I'm with you and that I love you.

Bailey smiled and put her phone away. Shana was the next to change and sat in Bailey's chair waiting for this show to get started. Bailey had everything she needed to begin working on Shana's hair. A big blast sounded and a voice over the loudspeaker said, "You may begin."

Bailey said, "I'm going to put my earbuds in. It helps me get into the zone." She started brushing Shana's hair and putting in the clips to bring all the hair to the center of Shana's head. Bailey moved right along, spraying it with hair glue and flat ironing it to stand up. Once Bailey was done with Shana's hair she moved on to her makeup. It didn't take as long as she thought it would take. Bailey applied foundation to Shana's face and outlined the wings around her eyes, filling them in with wild colors. Bailey brought her eyes to life as she added liner and mascara to the big eyelashes she applied. Bailey was going for a runway model, seriously overstated.

Faith and Ava stood back in awe to watch Bailey in action. Faith took out her phone and began to take pictures of Bailey working on Shana. When Bailey was done, Shana didn't look anything like she normally did.

"One more thing, Shana. I don't want you to button the jacket. I have these safety pins. Pin the jacket closed on each side and put this belt on." Bailey pulled a big chunky belt out of her bag. "Here I'll show you." Bailey crossed the bottom edges and pinned them into place. After Shana slipped the belt into place, the jacket now had a plunging neckline. Which showed off Shana's large bust.

"There, are you comfortable with showing off that much because we can close that a bit."

Faith said, "I think if you have it, you should show it off. This is a fashion show after all."

Shana looked in the mirror, "I still have my bra on. I think it'll be fine."

"Okay, Ava you're up."

Bailey began working on Ava's hair. Her style was a breeze because Bailey had it all worked out. The partial updo and the long twisted braid looked amazing. Periodically Bailey would ask, "How much time do I have?"

Shana said, "You have one hour and ten minutes."

"Good, thank you." Bailey kept moving. She no longer felt tired. Her adrenaline had kicked in. Bailey asked as she continued to work on Ava, "Faith can you put Shana's number on? The judges have to be able to see it."

"Ava's done, Faith your turn." Faith sat in the chair and Bailey went to town. Bailey knew Faith's makeup would take the longest. She quickly cut the suit and used wig glue to attach the nylon to Faith's face. Next, Bailey glued the mask to the right side of Faith's face. This was the tricky part. Bailey had to mix the liquid makeup to match the color of the suit so her skin, and the mask all looked as one. Bailey sprayed a little and had to adjust the color, but once she had it, she worked it. It wasn't long before Faith was completely purple. Bailey moved on to the fine details of the mask to make the ridges she put in it into scales. She matched the colors on the mask with the iridescent gems she added to Faith's suit.

"How much time?"

"You have forty-five minutes," Shana said.

Ava added, "Bailey, Faith looks amazing. Where did you come up with this?"

"You have to come up with something original because everyone looks on the internet to get ideas. I knew Faith liked purple, so I didn't think she'd have a problem with me coloring her hair that color."

Shana asked, "And the mask? Where did that come from?"

Bailey pointed to her head, "I had somewhat of an idea of what I wanted to do. When I found the gems for the suit, I tried to mirror it for the mask." Bailey kept moving.

Faith asked, "You are getting pictures of this, right?"

Shana said, "Yes, are you kidding me. This is crazy. I thought what she did with me was great, but this," She reached out her hand, "Is amazing."

Bailey started pulling small clusters of hair through the part covering Faith's hair. It made it stand up. "How much more time?"

"You have twenty-five minutes."

"I'm almost done."

"I know this is stupid, but can we help? I feel helpless just standing here."

"Ava, now is a good time to get dressed, because when that blasting sounds, we are done. I can't touch a brush or anything." Bailey said to Faith, "I'm sorry if I'm pulling too hard. I need to get as much of your hair through this hood thingy."

"I'm good. I want to win. So do what you have to do."

Bailey knew she was down to minutes when she thought she had all of Faith's hair pulled. She quickly sprayed it, gave it a tease, and sprayed it again. "Done." Bailey dropped her comb on the counter at her station. "How much time?

Shana smiled, "You have five minutes."

Faith said, "I want a picture of all of us." They found someone walking outside the curtain to take the photo. Faith and Ava stood on one side of Bailey and Shana on the other.

When the sound blasted and they said the time was up, Bailey let out a sigh. "I did it. Does everyone have your numbers on? Now we wait. The prejudges will come around and look you guys over. They then give the actual judges the heads up who to look at." Bailey pulled back the curtain and they waited.

Three people stood in the hallway and asked for each of Bailey's models to turn for them. It didn't take long for them to write on their pads and move to the next station.

Faith said, "They wrote down our numbers, I think. That's a good thing, right?"

Bailey said, "I don't know, but I really want to size up my competition."

It wasn't long before they announced numbers one to one hundred had to go to the stage. Shana was first to walk and her number was in the two-hundreds. So, they had some time. Bailey said, "Shana when it's your turn, be sure to have a lot of attitude. I mean be bold and out there."

Faith said, "Show it off."

When they called for the next hundred to go to the stage, Bailey walked with Shana and that's when she got her first look at other hairstylist's work. As Shana got closer to walking down the runway, Bailey's gut started to turn. Someone stood next to the opening and told people when it was their turn, "Go."

Bailey closed her eyes and tried to breathe. It was like two seconds and Shana was back. They returned to her station, and Bailey packed up her stuff. It felt like forever before it was Ava's turn. Bailey handed her a bouquet of flowers for her to hold as she walked. Once Ava was done they all waited for Faith's turn, and she didn't disappoint. Faith walked to the end of the runway, drew her gun, striking a pose as she leaned to one side, and pointed the gun as if she were scanning the audience. Then snapped upright returning her gun to her belt, and walked back.

"Oh, my God that was great, Faith." Bailey smiled so big. "I can't believe you did that."

"I thought if you were going to go through all this trouble to make me look like this. I was going to do my part and make them remember me."

Bailey felt a lot better when all she had to do was wait. But the fatigue was setting in. The night dragged on. One of the prejudges came to Bailey's station. "Ms. Mealey, please come with me. The winners have been chosen."

Faith said, "I knew you'd win something." Bailey gathered her stuff, and they all followed the woman. "Can you tell her what she won?"

"I'm sorry, I can't give you that information."

Bailey's stomach was feeling sick again. She pressed her hand on it to try to get it to stop. "I feel like I'm going to puke."

Faith put her arm around Bailey, "That's excitement."

Ava said, "Plus you didn't eat anything."

Shana added, "I have something that might help in my purse." But they were already in the staging area.

{16}

Bailey and all the other winners went out on the stage with their three models. Faith, Bailey, Ava, and Shana held hands. The Civic Center had thinned out, everyone that didn't win something had left, and all their spectators. So, everyone else moved closer to the stage. Bailey could see the O'Shea family sitting right up front with her parents. She tried to breathe and closed her eyes. *Tell me I'm not going to wake up and find out I missed the entire thing.* Bailey leaned into Faith, "Can you pinch me, so I know I'm awake? Ouch, thank you."

They started with honorable mention. You didn't win anything, but you knew you were close. A name was called out and they walked the runway. Next was fifth place for the Bold and Chic. Bailey's name was called, and the screaming and yelling began from the audience. Bailey and Shana walked the runway and returned to their place. They announced the other winners in that category and moved on to the Formal group. Bailey's name was called for honorable mention. Bailey and Ava walked and once again the cheers went up.

Bailey thought she wasn't doing bad and would be happy with what she got. When they moved on to Fantasy, her name wasn't called for honorable mention, or fifth, fourth, and third. But when they called her name for second place, Bailey nearly fainted. If it weren't for Faith holding her hand as they moved down the runway. Once they were back in their spots, Faith, Ava, and Shana started jumping up and down as they squealed. Bailey couldn't help the smile on her face. *I did it!* It didn't matter who won the best in show or first place. Bailey was happy with her first time out. She learned things that she'd change next time.

Once the fashion show was over, Bailey was dead on her feet and her stomach still felt queasy. But she managed to call Tane.

"I won Honorable Mention for Ava, Fifth Place for Shana, and Second Place for Faith!"

"Wow, I knew you could do it. Congratulations. That's my girl."

"Now, I'm about to crash, and here comes your family." Bailey got hugs from just about everyone, except Gabe and Patrick. Bailey noticed that Daniel wasn't there. She asked Ava, "Did Daniel come?"

Ava smiled, "I couldn't have him see me in my dress, now, could I?"

Tane asked, "Are you talking to me?"

"I'm sorry, it's crazy here. I'll call you when I get home. I love you."

Tane smiled, "I love you too." He could hear people talking to Bailey because she hadn't hung up. Tane sat there wishing he could have been there for her as he listened to everyone congratulating her.

Once again Bailey was feeling her lack of sleep. She couldn't be happier that the night was over. Bailey gave Faith what she'd need to remove the glue she used to attach everything to her face. Once Lauren took all the pictures and Bailey talked to everyone, she told her mother she was going home. "I'm sorry everyone, but I'm done. It has been a long day."

After Bailey showered and was tucked into bed, she called Tane. "I know I said I'd call but I'll apologize now just in case I fall asleep."

"We can talk tomorrow. I know you're tired."

Bailey sighed, "I'm beyond tired. For most of the night, I ran on adrenaline. A few times I could have fallen asleep. It was a night full of hurry-up and wait. I rushed to get everything done and then waited until each of my models walked down the runway for like two seconds. I hope someone videotaped Faith. She was great."

Tane knew Bailey had to be tired and yet she was still doing all the talking. "I will let you go. Sleep well, my Superstar. I love you."

"Me too," Bailey's voice faded.

Once again Bailey didn't hang up and Tane listened to her breathe as she fell asleep. He was in his bed in the dark and the sound comforted him as he relaxed.

When Tane woke, he and Bailey were no longer connected. Tane had some things to get done for school and he needed to clean his dorm room. That was his plan for the day. He had no idea when Bailey would call him. He didn't want to call her and wake her. Bailey earned a day to sleep in.

Tane went about his business, starting with cleaning his room. It wasn't all that big, but it sure got messy fast. He really needed to do laundry too. By mid-morning Tane was surprised he hadn't heard from Bailey. He pulled up her social media page and saw pictures Faith tagged Bailey in. Tane was amazed at how great Bailey did. He tried to text her.

Tane: Are you up yet?

He got no response. Tane figured she was still recovering from her long day and gathered his laundry to go to the laundry room. He kept his phone in his back pocket just in case Bailey tried to get in touch with him. *Maybe her parents wanted to take her out to celebrate.*

Tane put as much laundry into two washing machines as they could hold. He didn't leave the room because he'd be lucky if they just took his clothes out and put them on the floor, but most likely they'd steal them. Tane opened a book and sat down to read. There was no one else there and that was how he liked it. Going on Saturday morning was almost always a good bet. He sat back and tried to concentrate on the words on the page. Finally, Tane put it down and he pulled out his phone to call Bailey.

Tane listened as her phone rang. He thought he would have to leave a message. "Hello." Tane heard her scratchy voice.

"Hey, you sound terrible. What's going on?"

"I don't feel good."

"Did I wake you? You can call back later."

"No, that's fine," Bailey cleared her throat.

"Maybe you should see a doctor? I'm sure because you were run down you probably came down with something."

"It's Saturday. No doctor's office is open today."

"You can go to an urgent care. They're open."

"I might. I feel like I've been run over by a Mack truck. I puked a few times."

"You definitely need to go. Please, Bailey."

"I'm just so tired."

"Are you running a temperature?"

"I don't think so. It's probably a stomach bug. I didn't eat anything yesterday besides a few french fries."

"Bailey, that's not good," Tane sounded worried.

"I know, it wasn't on purpose. I didn't sleep the night before. I had to go to classes and went right to the Civic Center after school. Ava brought me something to eat but my stomach wasn't feeling good. I thought it was just nerves. When I got home, it took everything I had to shower and climb in bed."

"Can you get someone to take you to the doctor? Your mom, maybe?"

"I have no idea where everyone is. I know Louisa is here. She brought me something to eat."

"Did you have any?"

"I took one bite, and my stomach didn't like it."

"God, I feel helpless. I'd take you if I wasn't so far away. Call Ava, or Faith to take you."

"Faith doesn't have a car, and I've asked too much of them."

"Bailey, call my mom. I know she will take you."

"I'll try to get someone to take me."

"Text me and let me know what the doctor says." The two washing machines stopped and Tane had to put his clothes in the dryer. "I'm in the laundry room. But I'll be back in my room within the hour."

"I doubt, I'll know anything by then. My eyes want to close. I could just roll over and go back to sleep."

"Bailey, the doctors, then more rest."

"You're bossy."

"Only on the important stuff."

"Fine, I'll go."

"Be sure to let me know how you make out."

"Yeah, yeah, yeah."

"Bailey."

"Got it, boss." Bailey disconnected.

Tane shook his head when the line went dead. He put his phone away and moved his clothes from the washer to the dryer. Tane was truly beginning to hate being so far away. It wasn't like it would take hours on end to get home in an emergency, but it sure made him feel powerless. He knew if anything came up in his family someone would handle it, unless it was really important, and he'd have to fly home. But Bailey was almost on her own. Her parents both worked, and she was alone a lot. There was no way his mother would let any of her children stay in bed and not check on them without taking them to the doctors if she felt it necessary.

Bailey had Louisa but she wasn't Bailey's mother. *I guess Louisa is the housekeeper? Maybe Louisa raised Bailey, like a nanny?* Tane thought he could call Julia and ask her to check on Bailey. But Bailey might get mad that he sent her aunt to ensure she was alright. *Just wait to hear from her. Bailey said she'd contact me.* Tane found sitting alone unnerving, not that he'd speak to anyone if they were there. It had more to do with being alone with his thoughts and worrying about Bailey.

Tane pulled out his phone again, who should he call? He told himself to wait and pulled up Bailey's social media instead. There were more pictures from last night that people tagged Bailey in. Tane went through them one by one, and sure enough, there was a video of Faith on the runway. Tane turned his phone sideways so he could see it better and he smiled when Faith got to the end of the runway. He watched as she pulled her gun and made it look as if she would shoot someone. "Wow, I didn't realize how talented Bailey is. Faith looks great. I wouldn't even know that was her." Tane looked at every video and picture on Bailey's page from last night. Then he moved on to Faith's and anyone else's he could think of.

Tane sat there until the dryer went off. He slipped his phone away and gathered his clothes to take back to his room where he'd fold them. Once Tane folded his clothes and put them away, he started on his schoolwork. Every once in a while, he'd check his phone. Still no word from Bailey. He decided to text her.

Tane: Any word yet?

He sighed and went back to the paper he had to write. Tane's stomach growled, and he needed to get something to eat so he snatched his phone off his desk and went in search of some food. Time was passing so slowly. Tane tried to keep his mind occupied so once again he looked for any pictures from the fashion show. Lauren posted some really great shots. Tane texted Bailey again with no response.

When Tane returned to his dorm room, he decided to call his sister. "Hey, Ava. I was wondering if you heard anything from Bailey today?"

"Hi, Tane. I haven't talked to her. I'm sure she's trying to recover from yesterday. Why, is she not getting back to you?"

"I talked to her and she's sick. Bailey said she'd go to the doctors, but I haven't heard back from her. She thought she might have a stomach bug."

"Yeah, Bailey complained of her stomach bothering her a couple times yesterday. But she didn't eat, and I thought it was from all the stress she was under. It was amazing to watch her work. But doing three models in three hours, is crazy."

"I've been looking at all the pictures I can find. I hate that I couldn't be there for her. I'm so proud of her."

"What she did to Faith was incredible. That partial mask, and how she glued it and airbrushed it to look like part of Faith's face. Do you know she hand-sewed all those things on Faith's outfit?"

"I do because we were talking while she did that. Bailey did a ton of stuff behind the scenes. I give her a lot of credit. She worked really hard, that's why I'm not surprised she got sick. Did you know she didn't get any sleep the night before?"

"I know when we had to wait, Bailey was drained. She should have slept in the chair. We would have woken her when it was our turn to walk. Tane there was a lot of competition. Bailey did great. I can't imagine how the winner, overall, got all her models done."

"This was just Bailey's first time doing this. It could have been the third for the winner. I'm sure Bailey learned some tricks for the next time."

"Tane, can I ask you something?"

"Sure."

"Are you and Bailey together, together?"

"Yes, Ava. Bailey and I are together, together. I'm coming home the second my last midterm is done."

"Oh, do Mom and Dad know?"

"They know about school, and they know about Bailey."

"I figured they knew about Bailey. Mom was doing her best to make her feel comfortable at Sunday dinner."

"Yeah, Mom asked Bailey a few weeks ago and she didn't want to go. So, I can see why Mom was happy to see Bailey walk through the door."

"So, you see Bailey as the Sunday dinner material?"

Tane grunted, "Ava, Bailey is the one and only."

"Tane, you don't have any experience with girls, much less relationships."

"So, tell me how many guys you dated before you knew Daniel was the one for you?"

"Okay, I'll give you that, but I knew a whole lot more about guys than you know about girls."

"Why do you say you know more about guys as in men, and I don't know about girls as in children. Bailey is eighteen, and not that much younger than me. I know you might see her as a kid."

"I'm sorry, I misspoke. You have to admit, you know nothing about females."

"I'm sure learning."

"I don't think I want to know."

Tane laughed, "I'm sure you don't want to. I have to finish writing this paper. Thanks for talking to me and telling me about yesterday. I'm glad Bailey chose you to ask, you looked great by the way."

"Aw, thanks, Puddin' Tane."

"Don't call me that. I'm hanging up now."

When Bailey hadn't called or texted by dinner time, he was getting worried. But he didn't know who to call to find out what was happening with Bailey. He tried to call her and got her voicemail, "Bailey, I haven't heard anything from you, please call me." He waited an hour and tried again. "Bailey, I'm getting really worried about you, please call me." Next, he texted her,

Tane: I've tried calling and left several messages. PLEASE CALL ME!

Tane: Bailey, I'm starting to think something is really wrong.

Tane called his brother, "Hey Mack, is Julia with you?"

"Tane?"

"Yeah, I'd like to speak to your wife, please."

"You do know she has a phone, right?"

"Mack, this is important."

"Sorry, she's right here."

Tane heard his brother tell Julia he was on the phone. "Tane is everything okay?"

Tane sighed, "I'm not sure. I talked to Bailey this morning and she's sick. She was supposed to see a doctor and call me, but that was like eight hours ago. I tried calling her and left her texts. I'm getting worried."

"Alright, let me call the house and I'll call you back."

"Thanks, Julia."

It didn't take long for Julia to call him back. "I called and talked to my brother, and he said, Bailey went to the doctors, and she has some sort of stomach virus that has to take its course. Bailey's resting. She probably forgot to call you and fell asleep."

"Okay, thank you, Julia. I know how hard Bailey worked yesterday. She was feeling pretty run down. If anything changes, please let me know."

"I will, Tane. You know, while I have you on the phone."

Tane closed his eyes because he knew what was coming.

"I wanted you to know it wasn't that I disapproved of you and Bailey as much as I was concerned. I was worried that my niece would get her heart broken."

177

"It was a very troubling time for me. I won't go into details, but I was struggling with what I thought I wanted and what I was feeling. But I have no intentions of hurting Bailey. I love her."

"Okay, then. I…will call you if, you know, things change."

Tane felt a little better, but he wanted to talk to Bailey. He continued to try to get in touch with her on the off chance she might answer her phone. Tane had a gut feeling something wasn't right because Bailey didn't call him back. But he didn't know if he could trust his gut or not because he had all day to make up scenarios in his head.

Tane had to finish his paper and send it in. He didn't usually wait so long to get his schoolwork done. But thoughts of Bailey distracted him a lot. He never had something, or someone consume him the way she did. Tane sighed and had to trust what his sister-in-law said.

{17}

Bailey stayed in bed for the next two days. She pulled the covers over her head and didn't want to come out of her room. There was no way she wanted to talk to anyone. Bailey saw Tane's texts, and she knew he called a bunch of times, but she just didn't want to speak to him. She heard her phone go off again and picked it up off her bed.

Tane: If you don't call me. I am sending my mother over there to check on you. Bailey, it has been two days and I'm really worried about you. I can't get anything done. Please call me.

Bailey took a deep breath and dialed Tane's number. He answered on the first ring. "Bailey!"

"I'm sorry I haven't called you. I've been…" Bailey went quiet.

"What's going on? Are you okay? Is the stomach thing gone?"

Bailey pressed her lips together, "I have something I need to tell you."

Tane waited and it sounded like Bailey was crying. "What is it? Did they find something serious?" He felt his heart pounding. *God, please don't let her say something bad.*

"I'm afraid…you might get mad."

179

Tane thought why would he get mad? "Bailey, I've been so worried about you. I won't get mad...just tell me."

"I didn't have a stomach bug..."

"Okay, then what is wrong with you?"

"I'm..." Bailey closed her eyes, "I'm pregnant."

"Wait, you're what!? I thought you said..."

"I'm sorry. I didn't want to tell you. When I said I got my period, it was very light, which I do from time to time. The doctor told me I was spotting, and it wasn't a period...anyway. I'm eleven weeks. I'm almost out of my first trimester and I didn't even know I was...pregnant. My parents are going to kill me. Please say something."

Tane took a deep breath, "Let me see what I can do from my end."

"What does that mean? You aren't talking about getting rid..."

"Absolutely not. I mean give me a few days to get everything settled here and I'll be home. Did you tell anyone?"

"NO! I didn't want to tell you."

"Oh, Bailey. I don't want you to ever feel like you can't talk to me. But for now, let's keep this between the two of us. I'm going to talk to my professors and try to move my exams up. I might lose a few points, but I'm not worried about that."

"Tane, are you mad?"

"No, Bailey, I'm not mad. Maybe a little shocked, but we will figure this out. I love you."

"Like figure it out how?"

"Give me a few days and I'll be home. Bailey, this will work out, you'll see. Do you think you can pick me up from the airport? I don't want anyone to know I'm coming home until we get a chance to talk."

"Will you talk to my parents with me?"

"Yes, we stand together. You weren't in the pantry alone and it takes two."

"Tane, you have no idea how relieved I feel. I was so worried about telling you and how you'd react."

"Bailey, I was starting to think you had something seriously wrong with you, like dying serious."

"I don't think I'm ready for this. I still have to finish high school and get my cosmetology license. Tane, how are we going to take care of a baby much less financially support a child. You're in school and I won't be able to work at least for a little while after the baby is born. We're just kids ourselves."

"I'll have to put off school and work at the pub or work with my brother doing construction. Like I said, we'll figure this out. I don't want to cut you off, but I might be able to catch a few of my professors and see how soon they'll let me take my exams."

"Okay, will you call me?"

"Will you answer?"

"Yes, and I'm sorry about that. I needed a few days to…"

"Let it sink in. I get it. But you should have texted me and let me know you were alright."

"I didn't want to lie to you."

"Alright, I'll call once I know something."

Tane grabbed his phone and keys and went to find his professors. *Holy shit, I'm going to be a father.* He was sure Bailey's parents wouldn't take the news well, but he had to also tell his own. Tane's mind was going a million miles an hour. Who knew he'd be the one to come home with a pregnant girlfriend. Tane stopped walking, Bailey needed to be his wife...He didn't know how she would feel about that. They couldn't get married in the church, he couldn't ask that of his uncle.

One step at a time. You have to get home first. Bailey, my wife... somehow it felt right. She was eighteen and didn't need her parents' permission to get married. They would have to do it at the Justice of the Peace. The sooner the better Tane thought. It wasn't how he saw Bailey's wedding. He wanted her to be able to walk down the aisle in a white dress with her father on her arm. Bailey was his only child. That was something he could worry about later, Bailey hadn't agreed to marry him...yet.

Tane knocked on one of his professor's door. The door opened and Professor Klutz said, "How may I help you."

"Hi, I'm Tane O'Shea. I need to talk to you about the end-of-course exam."

"Please come in. You should know that I don't grant any extensions."

"Oh, I'm not looking for an extension. I have something going on at home and was hoping to take it early."

"Please have a seat," Professor Klutz put out his arm. "Is this a family emergency?"

"Of sorts, yes. It's not a life or death situation, but it is a family matter that I need to be home to take care of." Tane wouldn't lie.

"I can do that for you, but you will lose ten points from your grade."

Tane said, "I'm okay with that."

"What did you say your name was again?"

"Tane O'Shea." Tane watched as his professor looked up his name.

"I see you do very well in my class."

"Yes, Sir. I enjoyed being in your class."

"Very well, I will have my student aid contact you of the time and place. I suppose you'd rather take the exam sooner rather than later?"

"Yes, Sir. I'd like to be home in a few days. Thank you very much," Tane got up and shook his professor's hand.

Tane didn't get to speak to all his professors, but it was a good start. Unfortunately, it was going to take more than a few days and Tane wanted to be home like yesterday. He decided to email the rest of his teachers his request. Tane called Bailey back and told her how things went, "I'm sorry, it might take longer than I thought to take all my end-of-semester exams."

"Well, we have six more months to figure this out."

Tane held his tongue about his plans to marry her. This was something he wanted to ask her in person. "I wish I could come home right now."

"I do too. The last few days have sucked. I'm so hungry and then I smell the food and it's like, nope."

"What do they say, you're eating for two now."

"I can't eat for one at the moment. I can't believe I didn't know. I had no symptoms. I felt more tired, but I had so much going on. I just thought it was because of that. The doctor told me that's normal. I am growing a human inside of me."

"Did they do an ultrasound?"

"Yes, to see how far along I am. Our baby looks like a peanut with little arms and legs."

"Oh, I missed the first one, darn. Did they give you any pictures?"

"Uh, just a minute I'll send you what I have. I didn't even think about doing that before when we talked. There I sent them."

Tane waited for her text message to come through, "Wow, that's amazing."

"Our baby is about three inches long. Like the size of your thumb."

Tane held up his finger. "I need to do some reading. I don't know anything about having a baby."

"I need to make an appointment with my OB. I didn't want to do that until I spoke to my parents. I don't need them finding out when they get the bill."

Tane hadn't thought about that, who would pay the hospital bill? He took a deep breath, "Bailey, I want to go with you to the doctors, and I'll figure out a way to pay for everything. I don't want you to worry about it."

"Tane, remember we are a team. I need to get some more sleep. I'll call you tomorrow."

"Okay, you take care of the two most important people in my life. I love you, Bailey."

"I love you too, Tane."

The next day, Tane was able to line up two of his exams for the following day. He received responses from his other professors, and they also allowed him to take his tests early but with a penalty. Tane didn't care as long as he passed the class. At this point the idea that

Bailey was having his child had just started to sink in and he needed to be making real money.

Tane took two exams back to back the following day. He thought he did fine because he knew all the material. In three days, he'd be done with school and be on his way home. Tane started to gather his stuff to go home. He couldn't take it all but maybe after he married Bailey, they could come back in her car to get the rest of his stuff. Thank God, he only brought the bare minimum. Tane then went online and got his plane ticket for Friday. He used the money his parents had set aside for him to come home once the semester was over. Tane then messaged Bailey his flight details. He couldn't wait to see her.

When Tane took his final test and answered the last question he hit send on the computer the student aid gave him. "I'm done."

"Thank you, Mr. O'Shea. Enjoy your break."

Tane thought *this just might be a really long break.* He had no idea what was in his future, the career he had planned out for himself for most of his life was definitely not happening. After that change, his father asked what he wanted to do with his life and his answer was I have two years of school to figure that out. Now, he wasn't even sure he would return to school. He had a baby coming after all.

Tane rushed to get his stuff and get to the airport. Once he was on the plane, he sent a quick text to Bailey, telling her he was on his way. He sat back and closed his eyes. Tane thought about seeing Bailey. But he wasn't looking forward to telling his parents or hers. It was time to man up. He knew he'd get a lot of flak from his brothers for knocking up Bailey. Their words, not his. This was scary, but Tane knew God didn't give you more than you could handle. He had to have faith that this was how things were supposed to be.

When the plane landed, Tane was ready to get off. He got his bags out of the overhead compartment, slinging them over his shoulder. Everyone moved slowly down the aisle, Tane tried not to hit anyone with his stuff. Once he made his way out of the secure area, he saw Bailey waiting for him. When she ran toward him, Tane dropped his bags, and she jumped up into his arms. Tane pressed his lips to hers. It didn't take much to deepen the kiss. He wanted to soak her in. The months they spent apart felt like years.

"I've missed you," Tane kissed her again. He pulled back, "Let's get out of here." Tane returned Bailey to her feet.

"I can't believe you're really here." Tane pressed his hand to her very flat stomach. "I know, it doesn't look like there's a baby in there, but I assure you there is. I saw it moving."

"Come on, I want to be alone with you." Bailey took his hand once he had his bags back in place. They walked toward her car.

"I want to jump up and down, but it will use up too much energy and I'll have to take a nap."

"Have you been able to eat anything? I think you lost weight since the last time I saw you."

"Oh, I wouldn't be surprised. Food is not my friend right now. But I try to drink. Louisa has been making me protein shakes and they seem to stay down."

"You sound better."

"I'm starting to gain some strength back. I was really down there for a while." They got to her car and Tane put his stuff in her trunk. Once they sat in her car she asked, "What are we going to do?"

"Bailey," Tane took her hand. "This isn't very romantic, but I want to marry you. I want to know if you would do me the honor of letting me be your husband?"

Bailey's mouth dropped. "You want to get married?"

"Is this you buying time? Answering my question, with a question?"

"And you, answering my question with…"

Tane kissed her because she was talking too much. "Marry me." They were so close, he looked into her eyes. He thought he was dreaming when he heard her say, "Yes."

"I want to do it today. We can go down to City Hall."

"Wait, why today and City Hall? You don't want to get married in your church?"

"We can't get married in the church, besides I couldn't ask that of my uncle."

"Why can't we get married in the church?"

"One, it takes months to complete classes, and two, you're pregnant."

Bailey frowned, "I know people that got married in a church with big old bellies."

"You got pregnant out of wedlock, and my uncle will know that. I can't lie to him. I broke his trust when I put that code in the Parish Hall door."

"It's ironic, I can't get married in the church, but I got pregnant in the church."

"Well, it wasn't in the church where the altar is. I promise we will get married in the church."

"Wait, how are we going to get married in City Hall and the church?"

"When you get married by someone other than a priest and not in a church, you are not married in the eyes of God."

"Okay…"

"After the baby is born, we can be married in the church."

Bailey shook her head, "This doesn't make any sense."

"It doesn't have to, listen if we want to do this today, we have to tell our parents."

"I'm not looking forward to that. Right now, it's our little secret."

"I think we should go to my house first. My mom should be the only one at home. Once we get her on our side, we ask her to go with us to speak to your mother. Let your mother tell your dad."

Bailey took a deep breath and started her car. By tonight she and Tane will be married. Bailey knew Catholics didn't believe in divorce, even if they weren't married in the eyes of God. She would be Bailey O'Shea.

They pulled into his parent's driveway. It took them a few minutes to get out and walk to the side door. Tane used his key to let them in. He didn't want to scare his mother, so he called out, "Mom." They stood in the living room as his mother came down the stairs.

"Tane, Bailey what are you two doing here? Is everything alright? Is it Julia?"

"Mom, everyone is fine. We need to talk to you."

Arlene sensed something was wrong. Why was Tane home from school? She sat in her chair and Bailey and Tane sat on the couch.

"Mom, Bailey, and I have decided to get married. Bailey's pregnant." Tane was surprised when he didn't see any disappointment or disapproval in his mother's eyes.

"When?"

"Uh, the night of Paul's rehearsal…"

Bailey elbowed Tane, "I think your mother is asking when the wedding is."

"Oh, we want to do it today."

"Today? Why so soon…what about school…I have to tell your father…" Arlene put her hand to her forehead.

Tane said, "Mom we still need to tell Bailey's parents. Will you go with us?"

"Tane, why today?"

"Bailey is carrying my child, and I want her to be my wife as soon as possible." Tane pulled out his phone and showed his mother the pictures of the ultrasound. His mother's heart melted right there.

"Let me call your father and change my clothes. I will go with you." Arlene handed her son his phone and went upstairs."

Tane said, "I wonder what that conversation is going to be like."

"Yeah, your mother took it a lot better than I thought she would. Now, I don't see things going this good at my house."

"It's a shock, then as it sinks in and you realize how serious this is, and lastly you accept it."

"Is that what you did?"

"I was shocked, and I did realize how big this is, but as far as accepting it. There was never a doubt in my mind about what I was going to do. I just didn't want to ask you to marry me on the phone. The only thing I wish was different is how and where I asked you. I wanted it to be special for you."

"Tane, one day, propose to me the way you wanted to do it and where you wished we were."

Arlene came down the stairs, and they went to Bailey's house.

{18}

Bailey squeezed Tane's hand as they moved up the stairs to her house. Her mother was working from home today because she thought she caught Bailey's stomach bug. Bailey went to her mother's home office, "Mom, can you come out to the living room? I have something I need to talk to you about."

Her mother looked up, "Bailey, I thought you were at school.'"

Bailey turned and joined Tane and his mother in the living room. When her mother saw Arlene and her son, Bailey's mother asked, "What's this about?"

"Mom, you might want to sit down."

Tane took over, "Mrs. Mealey, Bailey, and I are getting married. Bailey is pregnant."

Robin jumped to her feet, "Oh, no. This is not happening. I will not have my daughter have her life thrown away because of one little mistake."

Arlene said, "Robin, I realize this is a shock, but Bailey is carrying your first grandchild."

Robin waved her hand in Arlene's direction, "I know you have your religion and all, but that doesn't mean we have to follow it.

Bailey is just eighteen. She has her whole life ahead of her. I don't want her married before she can even drink. I understand this will put a blemish on your family if they don't marry. If Bailey doesn't want to abort the child, she could always give it up for adoption."

Tane stood, "We are not aborting our child." He pulled his phone from his pocket and held up the picture of the ultrasound to show Bailey's mother. "Our Baby has hands and feet. Your grandchild is growing inside your daughter. Bailey is eighteen as you said. She really doesn't need your permission. This is more of a courtesy. Bailey and I will be married today. I asked her and she said yes. I know Bailey would be happier if you and your husband were there to see your only child get married. I," Tane put his hand on his chest, "Mrs. Mealey, would like you to be there."

Robin looked at her daughter, "Is this what you want Bailey?"

"It is," Bailey stood and took Tane's hand.

Robin sighed, "You know your father is going to have a fit. What are you going to do about school? Becoming a hairstylist?"

Tane said, "Bailey will finish school. I promise she will become a hairstylist. I will work hard every day of my life to provide for Bailey and our child. I will do whatever it takes to take care of my family."

"I hope you know what you're doing? I will call your father." Robin looked at her daughter, "There's no guarantees how your father will react to this news."

When Bailey's mother walked out of the room, Bailey turned to Arlene, "I'm sorry about what my mother said about your religion and your family."

"I understand your mother is upset, but we can't undo what is, we can only accept that this is God's will. This child may solve world hunger or cure cancer. We don't know and it is no fault of the child how he was conceived. So, we accept the things we cannot change."

192

Tane could hear the disappointment in his mother's voice although she didn't say so. Out of all his siblings who lived with their significant other, he was the one to get someone pregnant.

Bailey's mother came back in the room, "As I said, your father's not happy, but we can't stop you. When and where will the marriage take place? Your father and I will be there. We love you, Bailey." Robin hugged her daughter. "So, let me guess, that was no stomach bug you had?"

"Nope."

Robin asked, "What do we do now?"

Arlene spoke, "If it's alright with you? We can meet at my house, say in an hour. I think we will have a better idea about the where and when."

Tane, Bailey, and Arlene were back in the car. Tane said, "Thanks Mom, for your help. And I know you're disappointed in me. This is not how I saw Bailey and I getting married, but we love one another."

"Tane, it is not for me to judge. I had hoped I would get each of my children married before a child came. As you will see, God holds you responsible for raising your children. He wants you to raise them with God in their heart and to be a better part of society. Your father and I will help you in any way we can. We do not want to see you quit school, so therefore we would like you and Bailey to come and live with us. If that's what you want."

"Thank you, Mrs. O'Shea. I don't know what we're going to do."

"Bailey, I think it's time to stop calling me Mrs. O'Shea. You can either call me by my first name, Mom, or something else."

"What about Mama Bear?"

Arlene laughed, "We could shorten it to Mama."

"Mama it is. It's kinda funny, in a few hours, I'll be Mrs. O'Shea."

They pulled into the driveway and Cadman's truck was there. Tane felt a little nervous about seeing his father. He thought telling his mother would be hard but his father... Tane held Bailey's hand as they went inside. Cadman met them in the kitchen. Tane didn't look his father in the eye.

"Tane, come with me." Cadman put his arm over his son's shoulder.

Tane looked at his mother as his father moved them out of the room. He heard his mother ask Bailey if she wanted tea. They went out to the front porch. Tane wasn't scared of his father, but he didn't want to disappoint him.

Cadman rested his hand on Tane's shoulder. "Tane, I know your mother talked to you about staying in school, and we want that for Bailey too. What you are about to take on, I'm not sure you're quite prepared for. I know I sure wasn't. You're mother and I went through some troubling times and struggles. But we turned to each other and had our faith. You will be the man of the family, the one to make sure there is food on your table and a roof over their heads. That is a lot of responsibility, and it can feel crushing at times. I married a very strong woman who understood my struggles. It is important to be there for your wife as it is for her to be there for you. How you make a good team is knowing each other's strengths and weaknesses. You have to learn when to step in and when to hold back. These few months before you become a father, you need to build these bonds with Bailey because once this child comes, their needs come first."

"Dad, I know this isn't how I should have gone about this."

"Tane, listen to me. You are standing up, taking responsibility for your actions. What happened between you and Bailey is your burden alone. That is your cross to bear. It happened, now we move on. A child is a gift from God, and that is how we must look at this."

Tane began to tear up, "I'm sorry, I disappointed you."

Cadman pulled Tane into his chest and hugged him hard. "You are my flesh and blood. I love you with all my heart. There will not come a day that will change."

"I love you, Dad."

"I know you do, now let's go and make Bailey a part of this crazy family." Tane gave his father one more hug before letting him go.

It wasn't long before Bailey's parents showed up dressed for a wedding. Her mother brought something for Bailey to wear to get married in. Tane talked to Bailey's father and told him, he wanted Bailey to finish school and follow her career path. He promised her father that he would walk his daughter down the aisle one day.

Bailey's mother apologized to Arlene for her reaction to the news that her daughter was getting married and was having a child. Arlene told Robin she completely understood the shock of that kind of news.

All that was left was for Tane and Bailey to get ready to be married. Tane put on his suit and Bailey in her dress they went to the courthouse.

Arlene made a call to Mack at the pub, "Mack, your brother needs a best man. Meet us at the courthouse." The line went dead.

Mack looked at his phone. It was his mother's number. "Holy shit, who's getting married? I have three brothers." Mack went into the kitchen. "Ray, let's go! Have Herb finish the orders. Herb here's the keys, lock up after these last orders." Mack tossed his keys to the older man.

"Mack, what happened? Is someone hurt?" Raylan had panic in her voice. The last time something like this happened, Jon got hurt.

"No, it seems one of our brothers is getting married at City Hall."

"Who's pregnant?"

"Herb, pack up the food to go and tell them it's on the house. Let's go. I have to get Julia."

As Raylan gathered her stuff and her daughters out of Mack's office, she called Ava. "Ava, someone is getting married at City Hall. Bring some flowers. Call the rest of the clan."

Ava in turn started calling everyone. She had a good idea who was getting married. So, when she talked to everyone she said, "Tane's getting married." Each person she called agreed to call someone else. It wasn't long before the entire O'Shea clan had to make their way to the courthouse.

Tane and Bailey filed for their marriage license and then had to wait. Once their paperwork was processed, they were added to the list of other people getting married that day. Mack, Julia, and Ray were the first to show up.

Tane saw them and asked, "What are you guys doing here?"

"I heard my brother needed a best man." Mack hugged his brother, "Congratulations," he said into his brother's ear. Next, he hugged Bailey, "Welcome to the family."

Ray followed her brother's lead but didn't hug Bailey for fear she might get something on her dress.

Julia pulled a box from her purse, "Bailey, I want you to have this. It is my mother's engagement ring and her wedding band."

Bailey opened the box, "Aunt Julia, are you sure? You might want to save it for your own child."

"You are her first grandchild and I think my mother would be thrilled that you have it. Tane, here is my father's wedding band." Julia shrugged, "It can be a stand-in ring if you want to get something else." Tane took the ring from Julia and thanked her.

Julia's brother, Gary put his arm around his sister, "I agree, Mom would love to see her rings get passed down."

Ava was the next one to arrive. She held out a bundle of flowers, "You can't get married without a bouquet." Ava hugged Bailey, "You are so much part of this family." She turned to her brother, "Congratulations, Tane. I think you guys make a great couple and I hope you are happy."

"Thanks, Ava." Tane leaned into her ear, "Does everyone know?"

Ava smiled, "That's the O'Shea way. Nothing stays a secret, not in this family. Besides, we all want to be here for you."

The O'Shea family members started piling in. It looked as if fifty or sixty couples were getting married. When Tane and Bailey's turn came most of the O'Shea's were there. The judge's chamber wasn't very big, the family squeezed in.

The judge said, "Wow, normally I only have a few spectators."

The door opened and more family members rushed in. Everyone shifted to make more room. "Is this everyone?"

Tane looked over the crowd, "We are still missing a few." He noticed the absence of his uncle and wondered if he'd come.

"We have a few minutes to wait." The judge said, "You are the last couple for today. So, I hear you're the Fire Chief?" That's all it took for Cadman to start up a conversation to bide more time.

It took a while before Father Joe, Jon, and Paul walked through the doors, "We didn't miss it, did we?" Joe sounded out of breath.

Tane smiled, "We waited for you." He turned to the judge, "We can begin, my family is all here." It hit Tane that when he needed his family, they all stopped what they were doing to be there for him.

The judge said a few words and then allowed the couple to say their vows to each other.

Tane took Bailey's hands in his and made a solemn promise to love her and cherish her all the days of his life. Tane looked into her eyes, "Bailey, I want us to have a marriage that withstands the test of time. I want to be the one person you can always count on. The one you turn to when you need strength. I love you with all my heart. In front of all these witnesses, I will cherish you and promise to give you all I have."

"Tane, I give myself to you. I too, want to be the person you turn to when you feel overwhelmed, the one you can count on. I love you with all my heart. In front of all these witnesses, I promise to honor you and love you for the rest of my days."

The Judge said, "I pronounce you Husband and Wife. You may kiss your bride." Tane kissed Bailey for all the world to see.

Once the kiss was over, Father Joe said, "May I say a prayer?" He moved to the front of the judge's chamber. Joe raised his hands over Tane and Bailey, "Dear Lord, I ask that you bless this couple. May you understand their needs and help guide them. May you surround them with your love as they travel on this journey of life. I ask this in Jesus' name. Amen"

"Amen."

That was it, Tane and Bailey were now married. Joe reached out his hand and Tane shook it and then pulled his uncle in for a hug, "Thank you, Uncle Joe. I'm so glad you came."

"I wouldn't be anywhere else. I wish you and Bailey all the best." Father Joe turned to Bailey, "You are a strong young lady and I admire your spunk. It will take you far." He hugged Bailey, "When this settles down, I'd love to talk to you."

The O'Shea family surrounded the couple, and the noise level went through the roof. Bailey's parents worked their way to her and tried to have a moment with their daughter, but Tane's family was so overwhelming.

Arlene put her two fingers to her lips and let out a loud piercing whistle. "Everyone is welcome back at our house. I'm sure the judge would like to go home to his family." That's what initiated everyone to move out of the judge's chamber. He thanked Arlene and wished Tane and Bailey good luck.

Once they were alone, Tane pulled Bailey into his arms. "I love you, Mrs. O'Shea. Wait, that doesn't sound right."

Bailey smiled up at her husband, "I know, it sounds like you're speaking to your mother and not your wife."

"How about I say, I love you, wife?"

"I can't believe we're married. Do you know what that means?"

Tane looked into Bailey's beautiful big brown eyes, "It means I get to have you all to myself. We will fall asleep and wake up together."

"Now, where are we going to live? Your parents want us to move in with them and my parents want the same."

"Where would you feel more comfortable living? It's not forever. Just until we can get our feet under us."

"I don't know, I have a bigger bedroom than you do. But I like your house better than mine. Plus, I'd only have to go up one flight of stairs. But I don't want to hurt my mother's feelings."

"Well, we have a few days to decide. Ray handed me a piece of paper with a name of a hotel and a room number." Tane pulled the slip of paper from his pocket and a room key.

"Oh, wow. So, we won't be spending our first night married in either of our parent's house?"

"Nope, but we should at least make an appearance at my parents."

"I agree. But Tane, you have to remember it has been a long day with lots of ups and downs. I'm already tired. I know that puts a kink in the wedding night."

Tane picked Bailey up and she wrapped her legs around his body, "I will survive just as long as I get to hold you all night." He began to move them out of the building.

"No more teddy bear for me. I got the life-size version and I'm not going back."

Tane stopped walking, and moved some hair away from Bailey's face, "I didn't tell you how beautiful you looked today. I want you to know even though this is not how I saw us getting married, I knew we would end up here. That first kiss on my parent's couch, I knew. I tried my best to stop it, but you were like a freight train barreling down the tracks. You, Bailey O'Shea put a spell on me, and I couldn't be happier."

"Is that so? Are you calling me a witch? Whatever works. If I knew all it would take was one kiss, I would have done it sooner, and then bet you that you couldn't do it just once."

Tane smiled, "I would have lost that bet for sure. Now, let's get to my parents so we can leave and be alone."

"Sounds like a plan, Husband."

"I'm so glad you agree, Wife." Tane kissed Bailey.

Epilogue

Bailey and Tane went to his parent's house and the celebration was already in full swing when they arrived. It wasn't quite like being announced at a reception, but it sure did feel good. No one asked why they got married the way they did. Tane figured they all knew. There was no "That a Boy" as if Tane had done the deed. It was nice that everyone was there for him and Bailey. The champagne was passed around. Bailey and Julia had sparkling juice, as Cadman gave the toast.

"We gather here to celebrate this wonderful couple. We wish you all the best. To my youngest son, I say, put your wife above all others and cherish her. To my new daughter-in-law, I say, you are now part of this family, the good, the bad, and sometimes the ugly. We open our loving arms to you. You are now one of My Baby Girls, and I take my girls very seriously. May you flourish and bring many Godsends. It's a good thing we opened up the dining room." Cadman looked at his wife as she shook her head. "May God bless you both. Amen."

As the night went on Tane's family members gave him and Bailey cards. Robert slipped Tane an envelope and wished them luck. Faith's grandmother handed them a tin of wedding cookies.

When Bailey had enough, Tane said to everyone, "We would like to thank everyone for everything, but my wife has informed me, that she's ready to go. I love you all. I know I don't say it enough."

Someone yelled, "Yeah, I think that's the most I've ever heard you speak."

The crowd yelled, "Shut up, Gabe."

"Once again, thanks, Mom, and Dad on both sides. Thanks for all the gifts."

Bailey said, "I'm sorry. It has been a long day." She pulled on Tane's jacket. "We love you all. Bye," she waved as they left the house. Bailey handed Tane her keys. "You drive, I'm going to close my eyes."

"You rest, I got you." Tane took Bailey's hand in his. He rubbed his thumb over the back of her hand as he drove to the hotel. Tane parked in the parking garage and carried Bailey to their room. Once inside he brought Bailey into the bathroom. "A shower might feel good." Bailey didn't say a word as Tane undressed her and started the water. But then she said, "I need you to hold me up."

Tane realized what she was saying. He removed his clothes and stepped behind her. "I have you." Tane turned Bailey to wet her hair. He was going to take care of his wife and enjoy touching her every second he could. Bailey never opened her eyes. She completely relied on him to wash her. Once she was done, Tane wrapped her in a towel and carried her to the bed. They didn't bring any clothes, so he tucked her naked body in the bed and climbed in on the other side. Tane moved in behind Bailey pressing her body to his. "I love you, Bailey O'Shea."

Bailey mumbled something. Tane knew she was exhausted. He stroked her wet hair as he held her. It wasn't the wedding night most hoped for, but for him, it was great to have Bailey back in his arms again.

When Bailey woke and realized where she was and that Tane slept naked beside her. She rolled over to face him. He was hers to touch. Bailey placed her hand on Tane's chest, right where he had that patch of hair she'd been wanting to touch. Tane moved and she knew the second he was conscious because he smiled and covered her hand with his. He opened his eyes, and it was like looking into his soul. Tane had the O'Shea signature blue-green eyes. Bailey hoped their child inherited his color and not hers.

"What are you thinking?"

"I was just hoping our baby has your eyes. Your family has the most beautiful color eyes. I have brown, nothing special about that."

Tane caressed her face, "I like the color of your eyes. They are dark like chocolate. Was that all you were thinking about?"

Bailey smiled, "I was thinking how you are all mine to touch, like that hair on your chest. I've thought about touching you there ever since I knew you had chest hair."

Tane shifted her hand a little lower, "Anywhere else you want to touch me?"

"Oh, yeah," that was the end of their conversation. Bailey kissed him and Tane took over. They moved touching, loving one another. He got on top of her, and Bailey looked up at him.

Tane said, "Now, I will make love to my wife. We are as committed as it gets, and we are in a bed."

Bailey laughed, "And you don't have to pull out. I can't get any more pregnant than I already am."

Tane and Bailey came together as one and consummated their marriage. This was one of many times because they didn't leave the room. They ordered room service and enjoyed being together.

Once the weekend was over Bailey had to return to high school. She didn't tell anyone she had gotten married, she just kept it to herself. Bailey had missed a lot of school while she was sick and had so much to make up. The following weekend, they had plans to drive out to Tane's school to pick up his belongings.

Tane and Bailey were falling into a routine. They decided to live with his parents for the time being. They pushed two of his sister's beds together and used the bigger bedroom. But going to school and working at the salon took everything out of Bailey. She'd come home barely having something to eat before she fell asleep. The doctor said that should get better, but Bailey didn't think it was. She was starting to show, and they thought it was time to tell everyone.

At Sunday dinner, Tane stood. It was so not like him to address his family. "We have an announcement. Bailey and I are having a baby." His family just looked at him as if they already knew. "You could act surprised, you know."

Paul said, "I'm shocked it took you this long."

Mack added, "Who knew, my youngest brother and I would have a baby less than a year apart."

Tane shot back, "I can't help it if you are a slow starter." The ooh's went around the table. Tane never came back with a comeback.

Mack said, "Yeah, well I knew better."

"Apparently not. At least when my kids are in high school people won't think I'm their grandparent."

Mack started to laugh. "Wow, you have come out of your shell, haven't you."

"You started it. Anyone else got anything to say?" The table was quiet.

Arlene looked at her husband and he smiled. "So, now that you told everyone. Tell us what the doctor said."

Bailey said, "We know the sex. Does everyone want to know?"

"YES!"

Bailey smiled, "We are having a...boy." The guys at the table all were cheering, while the girls weren't so happy. "Sorry, girls. I know you want more girls in the family, but you just have to be happy with me."

Macy said, "I've got lots of boy clothes you can use."

Julia said, "After I get them right? I don't know if I'm having a boy. Mack and I want to wait until the baby is born." Julia was having a C-section because her doctor thought it would be easier on her back.

Ray said, "Well, God knows I've got the girl's clothes covered, times two."

Grace said, "Robert and I are expecting too. It's early so." Everyone cheered.

Tane said, "See, that's what I was expecting. That kind of reaction."

Gabe said, "You're expecting too?"

"I didn't mean I'm expecting, you imbecile. I'm married while you're still thinking about it. If you wait too long, you'll be in the same boat as Mack."

"Hey, I'm out of this fight." Mack waved his hand in Tane's direction.

"Faith has school, and I just got a real job. While you are married you still live at home."

Arlene said, "That's enough. No one should get married before they are ready. We are blessed with weddings and babies in this family.

Ava added, "I don't plan to get married until I'm done with school.

Lauren said, "We are still in the honeymoon phase. No babies to report yet."

Patrick uttered, "We are in no rush either. Shana still has school too."

Bailey said, "I have to finish high school. At least, I took my classes so once I graduate, I will have my cosmetology license. It's just getting to the end of the year pregnant."

Bailey was glad when Thanksgiving break came. It gave her a few days to catch up on some sleep. Although the O'Shea family did so much for the homeless. She tried to help, but for the most part, she was told to sit when she could.

After Thanksgiving, Julia went into the hospital to have her baby, and Mack was a wreck. As everyone gathered in the waiting room for word, Mack came into the room and announced they had a baby girl, and her name was Katlyn Michelle O'Shea. Michelle was Julia's mother's name. The girls in the waiting room cheered as the boys grumbled.

When the holidays rolled around, Bailey was struggling with being pregnant, going to high school, and being on her feet cutting hair. Tane rubbed her feet and back. "Bailey, have you thought about taking your GED? It would be one thing off your plate." Tane had been working full-time at the pub until he started back to school.

"I thought about it, and I have no doubt I'd pass but then I'd want to finish my hours in the salon. I'd be on my feet even more."

"What can I do to help?"

"Get me a rolling stool so I could sit on my big fat butt."

"Come on Bailey, your butt is no bigger than it was before, and there wasn't much there. I know because I've looked at it enough."

"My instructor does have me working the front desk to get me off my feet. It doesn't help my back though, and I'm not getting the experience cutting hair. I've even taken the pedicures, and I hate touching feet. They can be so gross."

Tane smiled because he was massaging her feet. "I want to make this easier for you. Do you want me to run you a bath so you can soak?"

"Yes, that sounds wonderful."

Tane went into the bathroom and started the water. He then went to his mother, "Mom, what do you suggest to help Bailey's back?"

"The heating pad is under the sink in the bathroom. She shouldn't put it on for too long and never sleep with it."

"I'm running a bath for her to soak," Tane headed for the stairs.

Arlene yelled after him, "You can't use it while she's in the tub."

"I don't want to electrocute her, Mom."

Cadman laughed behind his newspaper. Arlene said, "Well, you never know these days."

As Bailey got further along, she started feeling a bit better. Bailey took the test to graduate high school early and passed. She still did her six hours in the salon but because she didn't have classes in the morning it gave her time to sleep in. Plus, Arlene took her for better shoes. Bailey had been wearing an old pair of sneakers.

When Tane worked at the pub, she went with him and helped Raylan with the twins. The girls were getting bigger and didn't want to stay in their car seats anymore. Raylan bought a gate to put in Mack's office doorway and Bailey played with the girls. She took a nap when they did. It gave her a lot of practice changing diapers and feeding toddlers. Of course, she was only having one baby.

Tane loved wrapping his arms around Bailey's belly from behind. He talked to it and even read his schoolbooks to her stomach. Tane figured it couldn't hurt. He couldn't wait to meet the little person that grew inside his wife. The creation they made together. Part her and part him. Bailey made it into her second trimester and her belly was rounding out a bit. Tane loved to feel the baby move and sometimes it would get the hiccups. Bailey had a few more ultrasounds, which he thought was totally cool.

As time passed, the girls in the family planned Bailey's baby shower. She was in her glory with all the baby stuff. Bailey was now in her last trimester, and she was getting bigger. So, she started wanting everything to be ready for the baby, even though she still had a ways to go. Cadman helped Tane put the crib together. It seemed to make Bailey calmer. So, Tane did whatever to make her happy. They took their weekly trip to the baby store as their date night.

St. Patrick's Day was coming up and Bailey spent extra time at the pub helping Raylan with the kids. That was going to be her job while everyone else worked their butts off in the pub. She would have all the kids in Mack's office. It would be a lot because Bailey would have Bryant and Macy's two, Mack and Julia's infant, and Ray and Jon's two toddlers. She already talked Sean into being her big helper and of course, everything her big brother did, Callie wanted to do it too. Riley and Chloe were the two to get into trouble, and Katlyn would most likely sleep through most of the chaos.

The big day came, and Bailey showed up early. She knew it would only be Raylan's kids for a while and then as things got busy, she would have the other kids.

This was Ray's busiest day and yet she asked, "Bailey, are you feeling alright?"

"My back is hurting today. I must have slept wrong or something. You know how that is, right?"

"Oh, you have no idea. You think having one baby kicking you in the ribs is bad, try two."

"No thanks, I'll stick with the one I have. Tane told me how crazy it gets in here. So, I brought some movies for the kids to watch."

"That's a great idea." Ray sighed, "I love and hate this day."

"I'm sure, you do a lot of work getting ready and then getting all the food out."

"It helps a lot to know you have the girls. I wanted to ask you if you were interested in working the morning?"

"I... don't know if I could do it every day."

"I'd take what I can get. It's getting harder to work while they're here, but I don't want to put them in daycare. I guess it's something I have to think about."

"Sorry, I can't help you. Once this one comes," Bailey rubbed her belly, "I'm not sure how I'm going to finish the last few weeks of school to get all my hours."

"We need to open the O'Shea daycare."

Ray had to get back to work and Bailey went into Mack's office. The girls were in a playpen Raylan set up. "There's my Cutie Pies." Both girls put out their arms for Bailey to take them out. She took one at a time and put them on the floor. Bailey sat with her back against the couch and pressed her lower back into the bottom edge where it hurt.

When Tane got out of school he headed to the pub as he did since he became the dishwasher. He went in to check on Bailey. She was sitting on the floor playing with Chloe and Riley. He knocked on the doorjamb and Bailey looked up. The girls immediately got up and went to the gate for him to pick them up. "How are you doing, Superstar?" Tane had been calling her that since the fashion show. He picked up Riley and Chloe began to cry. Tane put Riley down and picked up Chloe, and the same thing happened.

"They aren't happy unless you have both of them." Tane scooped up Riley in his other arm.

"Tell me you don't pick them up together?"

"That's why you see me on the floor. I might have a hard time getting up but it's better than trying to get the two of them."

"Are you going to be okay with all the kids in here?"

Bailey reached over and picked up a few DVDs. "I brought some movies. So, hopefully, everyone will be calm."

"Don't try to do everything. If you need help, ask."

"And who is free to help me?"

"Bailey, you ask my mother, Ava. Someone will help you."

As it got later, Macy came with Sean and Callie. She also brought some movies. "Great minds think alike. Sean, I'm counting on you to help Aunt Bailey."

"Me too, Mama. We're her helpers to take care of the babies."

"Yes, you too, Callie Bear. Now, give me a kiss."

Bailey knew it was getting busy. She decided it was a good time to put on one of the movies. When Bailey got up her back was really hurting. She pressed on it to try and relieve the pain. The kids all climbed on the couch, and she sat on the end. Thinking the floor might not have been the best place. Bailey leaned forward and worked her knuckles over her lower back. But this pain wouldn't go away.

Bailey called out for Arlene, "Mama! I need you!"

Arlene appeared in the doorway, and right away she could see something was wrong. "Bailey, are you alright?"

"No, I have this sharp pain in my back and it's getting worse."

Arlene was over that baby gate and inspected where Bailey's pain was. "Ava, get your brother. I think Bailey is in labor."

"No, it can't be… it's oh…. too early. I still have…Ohhh."

Arlene said to the kids, "You guys stay here and watch the movie." She helped Bailey up. Tane came to the doorway.

"Ava said you think…"

"Ohhh, shit. My water just broke."

Callie said, "Aunt Bailey, that's a bad word."

Tane pulled the gate out of the way so Bailey could get out of the room. Ray yelled, "Did I hear her water broke?"

Arlene said, "Yes, we have to go. Get your father."

Cadman was there, "I'll get the car."

Tane scooped Bailey into his arms and carried her to the back door. Arlene opened the door for Tane and Bailey to get into the back seat. "Tane, it's too early. He still has over a month. Tane, I'm scared."

Arlene said, "Heavenly Father, hear my prayer. Please wrap your loving hands around this child. Give him all your strength and love. Let this child become one of your little lambs. In Jesus' name, we pray." Everyone in the car said, "Amen."

They rushed Bailey to the emergency entrance. Arlene yelled out, "We need a wheelchair over here." Tane climbed out of the car and bypassed waiting for the chair.

"My wife is in labor, her water broke. She's not due for weeks."

They took Bailey right back to labor and delivery. Tane handed his phone to his mother, "Call, Bailey's parents."

Cadman put his arm around his wife. Arlene's hands were shaking, and Cadman took the phone from her. "Robin, this is Cadman, Tane's Dad. Bailey's in labor. Yes, her water broke. Yes, we are here in the hospital. Okay."

Cadman guided Arlene to some chairs, "They are on their way."

"Cadman, I'm worried."

"The kids are in the best hands possible. You'll see. We'll have a St. Patrick's Day baby."

Bailey was already several centimeters dilated. There was no stopping this baby from coming. "How long have you been feeling this pain in your back?"

"It started a few days ago. I didn't think... oh, God that hurts. It's too early...I'm not due...Oh...damn."

"We'll take care of the baby."

Tane asked, "Can you give her something for the pain? That epidural?"

"It's too late for that, her contractions are too close together."

Bailey asked, "Where is my doctor?"

"We need to deliver, you're crowning. On your next contraction push."

Tane held Bailey's hand, he felt so helpless and to think his dad did this nine times, hell his mother. "Push!"

Bailey bared down and squeezed. Tane watched as his son's head appeared. "Come on my Superstar, his head is out."

"One more big push and his shoulders will be out."

Tane was amazed to see his son being born. "He's out!" He kissed Bailey's forehead, "You did it." The sound of the baby crying was music to his ears.

Bailey asked, "Is he okay?"

The doctor said, "They are checking him now, but he looks good. Small but healthy."

Once they did their tests and wrapped the baby up, they put him on Bailey's chest. Tane began to cry. He couldn't see straight. Bailey looked up at him, "Are you crying?"

"I can't help it. You did great. I stood here in amazement. We, we made this." Tane looked to the nurses, "Is he okay? He was born weeks early."

"We will do more tests in the next few hours, but he is breathing on his own and that's a good sign."

Bailey put her finger in her son's hand, and he wrapped his tiny finger around hers, "We need a name. I was thinking Lucky."

Tane smiled, "Lucky O'Shea. I like it."

After they settled Bailey in her room and took the baby for more tests, Tane went to the waiting room. He went straight to his mother and hugged her. "We have a baby boy and even though he was born early he's doing really well. We named him, Lucky. Lucky O'Shea."

Find me on the Web.

Facebook ♥ Trish Collins – Author

Instagram ♥ trish_collins_author

Twitter ♥ Trish Collins – Author @collins_author

Website ♥ https://TrishCollinsAuthor.net

Email ♥ TrishCollins.Author@gmail.com

Facebook Store ♥
https://www.facebook.com/TrishCollinsAuthor/shop

♥ Amazon.com/TrishCollins

Made in the USA
Columbia, SC
11 November 2023

25860719R00122